D0448007

SEP 2 4 2015

THE RED COLLAR

Jean-Christophe Rufin

THE RED COLLAR

Translated from the French
by Adriana Hunter

Europa
editions

Europa Editions
214 West 29th Street
New York, N.Y. 10001
www.europaeditions.com
info@europaeditions.com

Copyright © 2014 by Éditions Gallimard, Paris
First Publication 2015 by Europa Editions

Translation by Adriana Hunter
Original title: *Le collier rouge*
Translation copyright © 2015 by Europa Editions

Library of Congress Cataloging in Publication Data is available
ISBN 978-1-60945-273-5

Rufin, Jean-Christophe
The Red Collar

Book design by Emanuele Ragnisco
www.mekkanografici.com
Cover photo © ECPAD/France/Goulden, Auguste

Prepress by Grafica Punto Print – Rome

Printed in the USA

CONTENTS

THE RED COLLAR

CHAPTER I

At one o'clock in the afternoon, with the crushing heat over the town, the dog's howling was unbearable. The animal had been there on the Place Michelet for two days, and for two days it had barked. It was a big, brown, shorthaired dog with no collar and a torn ear. It wailed methodically, more or less once every three seconds, making a deep sound that was enough to drive you mad.

Dujeux had thrown stones at it from the doorstep of the old barracks block that had been turned into a prison for deserters and spies during the war. But that was no use. When the dog knew a stone was heading its way, it slunk back for a moment, then set off again all the more loudly. There was only one prisoner in the building, and he didn't seem to want to escape. Unfortunately, Dujeux was the only guard, and, being conscientious, he felt he couldn't leave the premises. He had no way of chasing the animal off, or of really frightening it.

No one ventured outside in this scorching heat. The barking bounced from wall to wall through the empty streets. Dujeux briefly considered using his pistol. But it was peacetime now; he wondered whether he had any right to fire a shot like that, in the middle of the town, even at a dog. More importantly, the prisoner could have used this as grounds to set the townspeople even more vehemently against the authorities.

It would be an understatement to say Dujeux loathed this particular inmate. The policemen who'd caught the fellow had formed a poor opinion of him too. He'd put up no resistance when they led him to the military prison, but smiled at them a little too sweetly, which they hated. He came across as so confident he was in the right, as if he'd agreed to come of his own free will, as if he alone could have triggered a local revolution . . .

Perhaps he actually could. Dujeux wouldn't swear to anything. What did he, a Breton from Concarneau, know about this little place in the Bas-Berry region? He didn't care for it, that much he knew. The weather was damp all year round and too hot in the few weeks when the sun shone all day. In winter and the rainy seasons the earth exhaled unwholesome mists that smelled of rotten grass. In summer a dry dust hovered over every track, and the small town, which was surrounded on all sides by open country, somehow managed—although no one knew why—to stink of sulfur.

Dujeux had closed the door and now held his head in his hands. The barking was giving him a migraine. With the lack of staff, no one ever came to relieve him. He slept in his office, on a straw mattress that he tidied away in a metal cupboard during the day. He'd had no sleep for the last two nights because of the dog. He was getting too old for this. He genuinely felt that, over the age of fifty, a man should be spared this sort of ordeal. His only hope was that the officer appointed to make the investigation would arrive soon.

Perrine, the girl from the Bar des Marronniers, came across the square morning and evening to bring him wine. He needed to hold out somehow. The girl handed the bottles through the window and he gave her the money without a word. The dog didn't seem to bother her, and on the evening of the first day she'd even stopped to stroke it. The locals had chosen their camp. And it was not Dujeux's.

He'd put Perrine's bottles under the desk and helped himself to them surreptitiously. He didn't want to be caught drinking if the officer turned up unexpectedly. He was so exhausted by lack of sleep that he couldn't be sure he would hear anyone coming.

In fact, he must have fallen asleep for a moment because there the man was in front of him when he woke up. Standing in the doorway to the office, strapped into a royal blue tunic that was far too thick for the time of year but was nevertheless buttoned up to the neck, was a tall man who stared down at Dujeux sternly. The guard sat up and, all fingers and thumbs, fastened a few buttons on his jacket. Then he rose to his feet and came to attention. He was conscious of his puffy eyes and the smell of wine on him.

"Can't you get that mutt to stop?"

These were the military investigating officer's first words. He was looking out of the window, paying no attention to Dujeux who, still standing to attention, was battling with a wave of nausea and thought it best not to open his mouth.

"Mind you, he doesn't look dangerous," the major went on. "When the driver dropped me off, he didn't move."

So a car had parked outside the prison and Dujeux hadn't heard a thing. He'd obviously slept longer than he realized.

The major turned to him and said a rather weary "At

ease." He clearly didn't put much stock in discipline. He behaved quite naturally, apparently viewing the military trappings of the situation as tiresomely quaint. He took a stick-back chair, turned it around and straddled it, leaning over its back. Dujeux relaxed. He would have liked a slug of wine and, with this heat, the officer might have been happy to join him. But Dujeux dismissed the idea and had to settle for swallowing painfully to ease the tightness in his throat.

"Is he in there?" asked the major, tilting his chin toward the metal door that led to the cells.

"Yes, sir."

"How many do you have at the moment?"

"Just the one, sir. Since the end of the war, it's emptied out a good deal . . . "

That was just his luck, poor Dujeux. With only one customer he should have been able to take it easy. But of course there had to be a dog and it had to howl incessantly outside the prison.

The major was sweating. He deftly undid the twenty or so buttons of his tunic. Dujeux realized he must have buttoned them up just before coming in, to impress him. The major was about thirty years old and, with this war they'd just had, it was quite common to see stripes popping up on men that young. His regulation moustache wasn't up to growing thickly and looked like a couple of eyebrows under his nose. His eyes were a steely blue, but they were gentle, and almost certainly nearsighted. A pair of horn-rimmed spectacles peeped out of a pocket in his vest. Did he not wear them out of vanity? Or did he want his eyes to have this unfocused look that suspects must have found unsettling during questioning? He took out a checkered handkerchief and mopped his brow.

"Your name, master sergeant?"

"Dujeux, Raymond Dujeux."

"Did you serve in the war?"

The jailer stood a little taller. This was a good opportunity. He could score a few points, override the sloppy way he was dressed and show that he took no pleasure in this position as jailbird-keeper.

"Indeed I did, sir. I was a chasseur. You wouldn't know now, I've cut off my beard . . . "

The major didn't smile so Dujeux plowed on with, "Injured twice. First in the shoulder at Marne, and then in the stomach, as we made our way up to Mort-Homme. That's why, since then, I've . . . "

The officer waved his hand to show he understood, there was no need to say more.

"Do you have his file?"

Dujeux hurried over to a rolltop desk, opened it and handed a folder to the officer. Its hardbound exterior was deceptive. There were in fact only two documents inside: the policemen's statement and the prisoner's military record. The major quickly appraised them. They didn't tell him anything he didn't already know. He stood up and Dujeux started reaching for the set of keys. But instead of heading for the cells, the major turned back toward the window.

"You should open this, it's stifling in here."

"It's because of the dog, sir . . . "

The animal was there in the full glare of the sun, barking insistently. When it stopped to catch its breath, its tongue lolled out and it was obviously panting.

"What is it, what sort of breed, do you think? It looks like a Weimaraner."

"With all due respect, I'd say it's more likely a mongrel. We see a lot of dogs like that around here. They're used to guard the flocks. But they're hunting dogs too."

The officer didn't seem to have heard this.

"Unless it's a Pyrenean Shepherd . . . "

Dujeux thought it best not to intervene. Just another aristocrat obsessed with hunting and hounds, one of those country squires who'd done so much damage during the war with their airs and graces, and their incompetence . . .

"Right," the officer concluded laconically, "let's get on with it. I'm going to hear what the suspect has to say."

"Would you like to see him in his cell or should I bring him in here, sir?"

The major glanced out the window. The noise the dog was making was no quieter. At least in the depths of the building the barking wouldn't be so intrusive.

"In his cell," he replied.

Dujeux picked up the big ring with the keys threaded onto it. When he opened the door that led to the cells a waft of cooler air came into the office. The breeze might have come from a cellar were it not for a hovering stench of bodies and excrement. The corridor was lit from the far end by a transom window that dripped a cold milky light into the darkness. The place was a collection of old barracks rooms, and heavy locks had been added to the doors to turn it into a prison. The doors hung open to show the empty cells. The last cell down at the end was closed, and Dujeux made a lot of noise opening it, like a walker thumping the ground with his foot to wake snakes. Then he showed the officer in.

A man lay full-length on one of the two bunks, his face turned toward the wall. He was motionless. Dujeux wanted to show a bit of enthusiasm and shouted, "On your feet!" The officer gestured for him to be quiet and to leave them, then went and sat on the other bed and waited a while. He seemed to be gathering his strength, not like an athlete preparing to launch and perform, but rather like someone who has to carry out a chore and isn't sure he will have the energy for it.

"Good afternoon, Morlac," he breathed, rubbing the bridge of his nose.

The man didn't move. Judging by his breathing, though, he clearly wasn't asleep.

"I'm Squadron Leader Lantier du Grez. Hugues Lantier du Grez. We're going to have a bit of a chat, if you'd like to."

Dujeux heard these words and shook his head disconsolately as he returned to his office. Nothing was the same since the war ended. Even the military justice system seemed hesitant, weakened, like this over-friendly young investigating officer. Gone were the days when convicts were shot without a by-your-leave.

The jailer sat back down behind his desk. He felt more relaxed, but didn't know why. Something had changed. It wasn't the heat, which actually felt more oppressive after he'd been immersed in the cool of the cells. It wasn't his thirst, which was becoming more and more intense, and which he decided to slake by cautiously taking a bottle from under his desk. In fact, what had changed was the silence: The dog had stopped barking.

After two days of hell, this was the first moment of quiet. Dujeux darted over to the window to see whether the animal was still there. He couldn't see it at first. Then, by twisting his head, he could make it out in the shadow of the church, sitting on its haunches, alert but silent.

Since the investigating officer had stepped into its master's cell, the dog had stopped baying relentlessly.

* * *

The major had opened the file and put it on his knee. He'd perched himself on the bedstead, leaning against the wall. It looked as if he planned on staying quite a while; he had all the time in the world. The prisoner hadn't moved. He still had his back turned, lying there on his hard bed, but it was obvious he wasn't asleep.

"Jacques Pierre Marcel Morlac," the major intoned monotonously. "Born June 25, 1891."

He ran his hand through his hair as he made his calculations. "So that makes you twenty-eight years old. Twenty-eight years and two months, as it's August."

He didn't appear to wait for any reply before continuing with, "Your official domicile is your parents' farm, the place you were born, in fact, in Bigny. Very near here, I believe. Mobilized in November '15. November '15? They must have deemed you were the family breadwinner, and that won you some time."

These presentations were an old habit of the major's. He trotted out the facts and figures with a sympathetic expression. The differences in dates and places that defined each individual were fundamental: It was thanks to them that soldiers were who they were. And at the same time, they were so trifling, these differences, so minute that they demonstrated better than any system of regimental numbers just how little there was to distinguish between men. Aside from these few jottings (a name, a birth date . . .), they constituted a compact, anonymous, indistinct mass. And it was this mass that the war had pummeled, wasted, consumed. No one could have lived through that war and still believed an individual had any value. And yet justice, which Lantier now served, required individuals to be brought before him for sentencing. Which was why he had to gather these scraps of information and stow them in a file where they would dry out like flowers pressed between the pages of a heavy book.

"First you were assigned to the supply corps in the Champagne region. That can't have been too tough. Requisitioning fodder from farms, that's something you know about. And it's not dangerous."

The major paused deliberately to see whether the accused would react. The figure lying before him still didn't move.

"Then you were sent off with your unit to join the Oriental Expeditionary Force. You reached Salonika in July '16. Well, at least this heat won't be bothering you too much! You had time to get used to that over there."

A truck laboring up the street trundled hoarsely past the basement window and drove off into the distance.

"You'll have to tell me about that campaign, in the Balkans. I never understood it at all. We wanted to give the Turks a hard time in the Dardanelles and they threw us back out to sea, is that right? Then we fell back to Salonika and played cat and mouse with the Greeks who couldn't make up their minds to join the war as our allies. Correct me if I'm wrong. Either way, those of us who were in the Somme always thought the guys in the Oriental Force were a bunch of draft dodgers taking it easy on the beach . . . "

In adopting these surprisingly colloquial terms and,

more particularly, making a genuine insult, Lantier knew what he was doing. His face still looked just as weary. These dramatic flourishes were always part of his interrogation routine. He knew which nerve to niggle in a man, just as a peasant knows the sensitive points on his livestock. The prisoner lying in front of him moved one of his feet. It was a good sign.

"Be that as it may, you distinguished yourself. Well done. August '17, a citation from General Sarrail: 'Corporal Morlac played a decisive part in an attack against Bulgarian and Austrian forces. He was in the front line for the maneuver and personally accounted for nine enemy infantrymen before sustaining injuries to his head and shoulder, and losing consciousness on the battlefield. He held on until his unit managed to get him back behind French lines during the night. This heroic action marked the beginning of a victorious counteroffensive from our troops in the Tcherna area.' Commendable! My congratulations."

This passage had certainly had its effect because the prisoner was no longer trying to pretend he was sleeping. Still lying full-length, he shifted position, perhaps hoping to smother what the officer was saying.

"It really must have been an act of exceptional bravery for you to be awarded the Légion d'honneur. The Légion d'honneur! To a lowly corporal! I don't know much about the Oriental Force but I think I've heard of only two or three similar cases in France. That's something to be extremely proud of. Are you extremely proud, Mr. Morlac?"

The prisoner was shuffling around under his blanket. It clearly wouldn't be long before he put in an appearance.

"Let's come to the act for which you were arrested. I can't imagine how a man who's won his Légion d'honneur in such circumstances could knowingly render himself guilty of what you've been charged with. I imagine you were drunk, Mr. Morlac? The war shook us all up. Sometimes the memories catch up with us and, to get away from them, we have a bit of a drink. A bit too much. Which can make people do things they regret. Is that it? In that case, offer up your apology, express your sincere regret and we'll leave it at that."

Facing the major on the bare boards of his bed, the man had finally sat up. He was swimming with sweat under his blanket, cheeks flushed and hair awry. But his eyes weren't bleary with sleep. He sat on the edge of the bed, his bare legs dangling. He smoothed one hand round the back of his neck with a grimace, and stretched. Then he looked directly at the investigating officer who was still sitting with the file in his lap and smiling wearily.

"No," the man said. "I wasn't drunk. And I don't regret anything."

CHAPTER II

H e'd spoken these words quite quietly, in a muted voice. He couldn't possibly have been heard from outside. But out on the square, the dog had instantly started howling again.

The major automatically looked over at the door.

"Well, at least there's someone who cares what happens to you. Is there anyone else who cares about you, corporal? Anyone who'd rather you extricated yourself from this regrettable affair and were free?"

"I'll say it again," Morlac replied. "I'm responsible for my actions and can't think of any reason to apologize."

The war had left its mark on him too, it would seem. Something about his voice implied he was hopelessly sincere. As if the certainty that he would soon die, which he'd experienced day after day at the front, had melted all the falsity inside him, all the carapaces, the tanned hides of lies that life and its ordeals and contact with other people lay down over the truth in ordinary individuals. The two men had this in common, an exhaustion that robbed all strength and any desire to say or think anything that wasn't true. But also, in among these thought patterns, any thought that related to the future, to happiness and hope, was impossible to formulate because it was immediately destroyed by the sordid realities of war. So all that was left were a few sorry sentences, spoken with the utter blankness of despair.

"Has that dog been following you around for long?"

Morlac scratched his arm. He was wearing a sleeveless undershirt which showed off his biceps. He wasn't actually very well muscled. Average height with brown hair, he had a receding hairline and light-colored eyes. He was obviously a country type but there was an inspired look about him, an intensity in his eyes that might be associated with a prophet or a shepherd visited by apparitions.

"Since forever."

"What do you mean?"

Lantier was starting to write a report of the interrogation. He needed precise details to complete the exercise. But he did it without any enthusiasm.

"He followed me when they came to call me up to war."

"Tell me about that."

"If I can smoke."

The major rummaged in his vest and took out a crumpled pack of cigarettes. Morlac lit one with the tinder lighter the officer handed him. He blew the smoke through his nose like an enraged bull.

"It was late autumn. You know all this; it's in your papers. We still had plowing to do. My father hadn't been well enough to follow the horses for a long time. And I also had to do the neighbors' fields, because their son had been among the first to go. They came in the middle of the day, the police. I saw them coming up the line of linden trees and I just knew. My father and I had talked about what I should do. I was all for hiding. But he knew them and he said they'd get me sooner or later. So I went along with them."

"Were you the only one they had to get?"

"Of course I wasn't," he said quietly. "They already had three other conscripts with them. Men I knew by sight. The police got me to climb into their cart and then we went and picked up three more."

"And the dog?"

"He followed."

Did the animal hear that? He hadn't stopped barking since his master woke up, but now he was being discussed he was silent.

"He wasn't the only one actually. All the others had dogs that followed them in the early days. The cops laughed. I think they deliberately made them run behind the cart. It made it feel kind of cheerful, like going off for a day's hunting. So the guys we went to fetch let themselves be loaded into the cart without a scene."

He described all this with laughter in his voice but his eyes were still sad, and sitting facing him, the officer displayed the same superficial brightness.

"Had you had the dog long?"

"Some friends gave him to me."

The major noted everything down scrupulously. There was something slightly comical about the way he earnestly recorded this business about a dog. But the animal did play an important role in the affair he'd come to investigate.

"What breed is it?"

"The bitch was a Briard Sheepdog, pretty much purebred as I understand it. No one really knows about the dog. Apparently every male in the neighborhood had a shot at her."

There was nothing lewd about what he was saying, more a sense of disgust. It was strange how the war had made anything carnal like this unbearable. As if this magma surrounding our origins, these mysteries of reproduction, were tragically correlated to the orgy of blood and death, the hideous scramble that the shelling had produced in the trenches.

"Anyway," the officer interjected, "the dog followed you and then what?"

"Then he carried on. He was craftier than the others, I s'pose. We were rounded up in Nevers, and from there we caught a train for the East. Most of the dogs stayed on the platform, but not this one, he crouched down and as the train set off, he leapt onto the flat car."

"Didn't the NCOs drive him away?"

"It made them laugh. If there had been thirty of them they'd have chucked them out, but just one, they quite liked it deep down. He became the regimental mascot. At least that's what they called him."

The two men were now facing each other, each on a board bed, separated by the narrow confines of the cell. It felt a bit like during the war, in the blockhouses. There was plenty of time. Life dawdled by and yet a shell could end it all at any moment.

"And *you* obviously liked it. Were you attached to your dog?"

Morlac delved thoughtfully inside the pack of cigarettes. He drew out one that was half broken, snapped it in two and lit one of the ends.

"You might think this is strange, especially with what I've just done, but I've never felt very strongly about dogs. I don't like hurting animals; I take care of them if need be. But if need be I'll kill them, too, with rabbits and sheep for example. With a dog, I'll take it hunting or into the fields to watch over the cows. But stroking it and all that, that's not really my style."

"Weren't you happy he followed you?" Lantier asked, looking up.

"To be honest, it was more like I was embarrassed. I didn't want to be noticed, in that whole war thing. Especially at the beginning. I didn't know how things would turn out but I kept thinking that at some point I might need to slip away so, with a dog . . . "

"You wanted to desert?"

Lantier wasn't asking the question as an investigator, more as an officer, one who thought he knew his men and finds a character trait he wasn't expecting in one of them.

"I think you may have been prepared for what war would be like. I wasn't. In the early days what I mostly saw were the fields left behind to my mother and my sister, who couldn't work them, and the hay that hadn't been brought in. So I thought if I wasn't needed that badly by the army, I'd try to get back to where I was useful. Do you understand?"

The officer was a city dweller. He'd been born in Paris and had always lived there. He'd often noticed amongst his men how differently those from towns and those from the country viewed the home front. To a townie, home meant pleasure and comfort—laziness, basically. To a peasant, home was the land and work, a different battle.

"Were there other dogs in your convoy apart from yours?"

"Not in the train. But in Reims, when we got off, we found quite a few."

"Didn't your officers say anything?"

"There wasn't anything to say. The dogs looked after themselves. I don't know if they were going through the garbage at night or if people threw them scraps. Both, probably. Anyway, they didn't need looking after."

"Then did you go to the front?" Lantier moved the interrogation forward.

"I stayed there six months in the supply corps. We weren't on the front line but sometimes we came very close and the shells often took their toll."

"And was the dog still with you?"

"Still with me."

"That's pretty remarkable."

"He's a remarkable dog," Morlac replied steadily. "Even in the most ravaged landscapes he always managed to find something to eat. The main thing was he knew what to do around the officers. Most of the dogs ended up having problems. There were even some that were unceremoniously eliminated with a rifle shot because they stole from the stores. I don't know where you were but you must have seen that, too."

During conversations in the trenches it was sometimes possible to forget issues of rank like this. It was rather like those card games where a road-mender can rail at a notary without anyone taking offense. Inside that cell, the investigating officer remained an investigating officer, carefully writing his report, but the interrogation was also a conversation between fellow soldiers who would soon be leveled by death.

"I spent most of the war with the English in the Somme," said the officer.

"Were there any dogs?"

"A few. In fact, when I was given your case I immediately remembered several of my own men who became so attached to their dogs it was only thanks to them they could cope with the war at all. They ended up thinking of them as brothers-in-arms, alter egos. To tell you the truth, and despite your provocative comments, I intend to draft my statement in those terms. At the end of the day you established a connection with this dog as a comrade-in-arms. Put like that, you'll get a pardon, I'm sure of it."

Morlac straightened and hurled his cigarette against the wall at the far end of the cell. He looked furious. The war, which had deprived him of the softer facial expressions associated with joy and pleasure, had clearly developed his capacity to express anger and even loathing. The officer was familiar with reactions like this from soldiers but he hadn't expected it in this instance and, more significantly, couldn't work out the grounds for it.

"I don't want you to write that, do you hear me!" Morlac shouted. "It's not true, it's just not true."

"Easy, easy! What's gotten into you?" Lantier asked with an ill-tempered sigh.

"I didn't do what I did because I love my dog. Exactly the opposite in fact."

"Don't you love him?"

"This isn't about whether or not I love him. I didn't do it for him, I tell you."

"Who for, then?" Lantier looked him in the eye.

"Who for? Well, for you, how about that, for the officers, the politicians, the profiteers. And for all the idiots who follow them, who send others off to war, and also for the ones who actually go. I did it for everyone who believes in that claptrap: Heroism! Bravery! Patriotism!"

He'd risen to his feet as he shouted these last few words. The blanket had fallen to the floor and he was just in his underwear as he stood there yelling, scowling at the officer. He looked ridiculous and pathetic but also worrisome, because there was a palpable sense that his anger could drive him to extreme acts, and nothing and no one could stop him from completing them.

After a brief stunned silence, Lantier recovered his officer's instincts. He snapped the file shut, stood up very straight and, with all the authority readily available to a clothed man—and, what's more, in uniform—before a naked man, he said forcefully, "Calm down, Morlac! You're overstepping the line. Don't overestimate my good nature. It has its limits."

"You want me to talk, I'm talking."

"And what you're saying is unacceptable. You're aggravating your situation. Not only have you failed to mitigate the gesture that brought you here, but you're compounding it with insults to an officer and dishonor to the nation."

"I've already sacrificed too much for it, for the nation. That gives me the right to tell it a few home truths."

He wasn't backing down. Disheveled as he was, Morlac was squaring up to the investigating officer and answering him back. That was what four years of war had produced: men who were no longer afraid, who'd survived so many horrors that nothing and no one could make them look away. Luckily, there weren't too many of them. Lantier knew it was better to cut this short than continue a discussion that undermined the authority he represented.

"You pull yourself together, old boy. We'll leave it at that for today."

Dujeux, the jailer, must have come over when he heard raised voices. He popped out from behind the door, threw a thunderous look at Morlac, and escorted the officer away, clanking his keys along the metal doors as he walked.

Outside, the dog had started baying again.

* * *

Lantier du Grez had offices in Bourges, right in the town center in the Louis XIV building that the locals called the Condé Barracks. He liked it well enough, until something better came along. His wife had stayed in Paris with their two children, and he was hoping for a transfer so he could go home to them at last.

Until he had finished investigating the Morlac case, there was unfortunately no question of him returning, either to Bourges or to Paris. For the duration of his inquiry he had taken lodgings in a modest hotel for traveling salesmen, near the station. The brass bed creaked and the towels were threadbare. The only pleasant time in the establishment was breakfast. The owner, who was a war widow, kept a farm with her sister on the outskirts of town. The butter, milk and eggs came from this farm. She baked her own bread and made her own jams.

At half past seven in the morning it was already obvious it would be a hot day. Lantier had breakfasted by a wide-open window. He thought about this wretched man and his dog. Truth be told, he hadn't stopped thinking about him since the previous day.

He'd had to leave him abruptly. He couldn't allow himself to be insulted, taking into account what he represented. But personally, he was peculiarly fascinated by this stubborn little character.

During the course of that endless war, Lantier had been through every kind of emotion. He'd started out as a young idealist typical of his social standing (solidly middle-class despite the lesser nobility suggested by his family name). All that mattered at first was his country and the high-blown ideals that went with it: Honor, Family, Tradition. He thought individuals and their pitiful personal interests had to be subjugated for their sake. And then, in the trenches, he'd lived at close quarters with these individuals, and had sometimes taken their side. Once or twice he'd reached the point where he wondered whether their suffering was owed more respect than the ideals in whose name it was inflicted on them.

After the armistice, Lantier saw his appointment to the military justice system as serendipity. The relevant committees must have felt he was ripe for this difficult responsibility: protecting the military institution, defending the interests of the nation and also understanding men's failings.

But this prisoner was different. He belonged in both camps: he was a hero, he had defended his country, yet at the same time he loathed it.

Lantier spent the whole morning strolling about town. He'd stopped at a bistro outside the abbey-church, and had organized the notes he'd taken the previous day in the prison.

He didn't intend to see Morlac again before the afternoon. He had to give him time to calm down and think, even if he didn't really believe Morlac would.

When the church bell struck noon, the streets were in a state of complete torpor. Lantier cut across town to have lunch in a restaurant he'd spotted near the covered market. The shutters were closed on all the houses to keep the rooms cool. Behind metal doorways he heard women's voices and the clink of plates coming from gardens: People were getting ready to eat outside.

The restaurant was deserted, except for one table at the back where an elderly man was seated. Lantier du Grez settled himself at the far end of the banquette, toward the window. The room had a high ceiling with stucco yellowed by grease on the walls and tall, badly flaking mercury mirrors. The owner had wound the canvas awning down over the terrace and opened everything he could—windows, doors, transoms—to create a draft. But the steam laden with a smell of frying that came up from the kitchen defeated all these efforts, and it was very hot.

The food on offer was the same all through the year, essentially comprising hearty dishes suitable for rainy weather. Lantier ordered rabbit chasseur, hoping against his better judgment that the sauce wouldn't be too fatty.

He asked for a newspaper and the owner brought him one that was two days old. He read the headlines, which were mostly about the prowess of the aviator Charles Godefroy, who'd flown his plane under the Arc de Triomphe.

"You're here for Morlac, aren't you?"

Lantier looked over at the old man who'd called across to him. The latter rose slightly from the banquette with a sketchy wave of the hand.

"Norbert Seignelet, attorney-at-law."

"My pleasure. Major Lantier du Grez."

There'd been an attorney-at-law in his section when he was a lieutenant. He'd been a punctilious, self-righteous character, always negotiating interpretations of the law in order to do as little as possible. And yet, with the first offensive, he'd climbed out of the trench before the others and was killed within two yards of the parapet.

"I am indeed here to investigate the Morlac case. Do you know the man?"

"Sadly for me, Major Lantier, I know everyone in this town, in the whole region, even. That's what happens with my line of work and my age. I should add that in my family we've been exercising the same duty for five generations."

Lantier nodded, but, as his rabbit had arrived steaming, he busied himself spooning the meat from the earthenware serving dish, careful not to take too much sauce.

"When I saw him go past with his dog in the Bastille Day parade, I would never have imagined . . . " the attorney said, adopting a cautiously comical expression which could have evolved into indignation or an unabashed smile, depending on the route Lantier adopted. But the latter, who had tucked into his rabbit, chose not to help him out.

"And what did you think of what he did?"

The older man screwed up his eyes and looked at Lantier evasively.

"I was surprised. I wasn't expecting that from him."

"What do you know of Morlac?"

"Before the war he was just an ordinary man. I knew the family by sight. The father was a plowman, very pious, very hardworking. He and his wife had eleven children but only two survived, this Jacques who's in prison and Marie, a sister four years younger. They're both scrawny things by the looks of them. But don't pay any attention to that. They're the ones that survived."

"Did he have any education?"

"Not much. That's not the custom in these parts, especially when there aren't many children in the family. The parish priest gave him lessons, so he could read and count. Then he went out in the fields to help his father."

Lantier nodded but was actually mostly preoccupied trying to get shards of shattered bone from his meal out of his mouth. He didn't like thinking about how the animals he ate had been killed. In this instance, though, he couldn't help it.

"No friends? No political leanings?"

"He knew a few other young men in the area. He'd see them on market days and sometimes at a dance, not that he went very often. As for politics, it's pretty quiet around here, you know. People vote the same way as their priests. Oh, there's a handful of agitators, particularly teachers and railroad men, and they get together in a café over by the station. Near your hotel, actually."

"So you know which hotel I'm staying in?"

The attorney shrugged and didn't bother to give any reply but a smile.

"And since he came home from the war?"

"We hardly knew he was here, except for that infamous day . . . He'd taken furnished lodgings. His sister's married and he doesn't really like his brother-in-law, so he hasn't set foot back on the farm. But that's hardly surprising. Lots of war veterans have gone completely feral."

The officer took this comment personally. After all, he was a war veteran, too. And if he thought about it, he had to admit he hardly saw anyone now and people must have found some of his behavior strange.

"Does he have a wife?"

"That's a mystery. He never lived with anyone. But in a small village not far from here there's a girl who people claimed, for a while, was his sweetheart. You know what it's like: people talk, but where's the truth in that?"

"What is her name?"

"Valentine. She lives on the edge of the village of Vallenay."

"Does she have family?"

"No, they all died in a measles epidemic. She inherited a small property that she's put out to a tenant farmer. It brings in a bit for her, and she makes wicker baskets. Oh, I was forgetting. She has a child."

"Of what sort of age?"

"Three, I think."

"Is it Morlac's?" Lantier couldn't help asking.

"No one knows."

"But he was at war . . . "

"He came home on leave."

Lantier had almost finished his rabbit. What with the sauce and the heat, he was breaking out in a sweat. He unbuttoned his vest and mopped his face. The next few hours were going to be unbearable. It would be better to go back to the hotel, lie down and sleep.

The attorney didn't have much more to tell him but he wanted to be rewarded for these confidences with military secrets. He could have spared himself the trouble, though, because Lantier paid for his meal with a yawn, and took his leave without putting his jacket back on.

CHAPTER III

By the time the rabbit chasseur had settled, it was four o'clock in the afternoon and Lantier, still smeary-faced, left the hotel and headed for the prison. He now knew the town well enough to take the shortcut and get to the former barracks without doubling back on himself.

At first he thought the dog had stopped barking. But that was because he was coming along a different street, at the back of the building. When he turned the corner, he heard it. It seemed to him the animal wasn't howling so loudly. No doubt the exhaustion. The jailer told him that in three days the dog had only stopped once, during his own visit the day before.

"Does he bark at night too?"

"At night, too," Dujeux confirmed, rubbing his eyes that were puffy with insomnia.

"And haven't people in the neighborhood said anything?"

"First of all, not many people live around here. But also I think that, with all due respect to you, sir, people don't view the military in a very good light in these parts. Of course, they say they're proud of our marshals and they're all praise for the soldiers. But they also remember the military police came to dig them out from their farms, and officers shooting those who weakened. You have to realize that for four years this prison was full of men going before court-martials because they'd tried to hide."

"Are you telling me people are siding with Morlac?"

"Not with him in particular, but, you see, he's the last prisoner. And this business with the dog, it's softened everyone. At night I've seen shadows sneaking over to give the mutt food."

The officer asked to be shown into Morlac's cell. This time the man was not asleep. He was dressed and reading, sitting on the floor to make the most of a ray of sunlight filled with dust motes that cut across the cell.

"You look as if you've calmed down. We can carry on, then."

Lantier sat in the same place as the day before, on one of the bedsteads.

"Sit yourself opposite me, would you."

The prisoner rose slowly, put his book down on the edge of the bed and sat down. In his civilian clothes he looked less like a lunatic visited in the hospital.

"What are you reading? Can I see?"

The officer leaned forward to take the book. It had worn corners, and the edges of the pages were curled. It must have been carted around in many a pocket and been caught in the rain several times.

"Victor Hugo, *Han d'Islande*."

Lantier looked up and peered at the stubborn little peasant who sat before him. He thought he could see a smile on his lips. But the man immediately reverted to his sulky defendant's expression with surly, staring eyes.

"I thought you hadn't been to school."

"That's my school," Morlac replied, tilting his chin toward the book. "And the war, too."

The officer put the book down and wrote something in his notebook. He didn't feel very comfortable continuing the investigation on this territory. As far as literature was concerned, he liked the Greeks and Cicero, Pascal and the classics. The only contemporaries he'd read were those who glorified France, particularly Barrès. In his works, there was veneration for both the monarchy and the Empire—in other words, authority. And there was scorn for the Republic, for which Victor Hugo was the bard.

"Let's pick up where we left off," said Lantier, going over his notes. "You were in Champagne. Did you have any leave in the six months you were there?"

"Yes."

"And did you come here?"

"Yes."

"With your dog?"

"No, he waited for me there. The boys looked after him."

"Then you were posted with the Oriental Expeditionary Force," Lantier said, checking the file. "And did he follow you there?"

"First my regiment went down to Toulon by train. The dog came with us. But I was convinced he wouldn't go further than that. So long as we were in billets, things were still okay for him. But the port was different. In their dockyard the naval riflemen waged war on animals and didn't think twice about shooting them. We'd only been in the docks two days when the dog disappeared."

"Did you board a military vessel?"

"No, a requisitioned cargo ship: the *Ville d'Oran*. It was

an old tub covered in rust which had shuttled backward and forward to the colonies before the war. We stayed onboard for four days before casting off. It smelled of palm oil and droppings because there were about fifty horses in the hold, for the officers. Everyone was sick and we hadn't even put out to sea yet."

"And was the dog onboard?"

"We didn't know right away. That's what's amazing about it. He must have realized that, so long as we were still on the quay, he shouldn't show his face. He came out of hiding on the second day of the crossing."

"And didn't the officers throw him overboard?"

"Officers? We never saw them," Morlac hissed, eyeing the major with the surly look in his eye again. "They were in the wardroom, with the captain, probably to avoid being on view when they puked."

"The NCOs, then?"

"He's crafty, that dog, I've told you that. When he showed up, he had a rat between his jaws. In those four days we'd had time to see there was a lot of vermin on the ship, so everyone was pleased he'd come to sort things out a bit in the hold."

"And did he become the regimental dog?"

"No, because he didn't see himself like that. He always knew he was my dog. He lay at my feet, slept by my side, and if anyone came up to me looking for trouble, he growled."

There was something strange about the tone Morlac had adopted. He was willingly talking about the dog in favorable terms. But there was no detectable warmth in his voice. More like contempt or regret. It was as though he passed harsh judgment on the qualities he was describing.

"Did you give him a name?"

"Not me. The others did. Since he'd jumped on the train, the boys called him Wilhelm, for a laugh. Because of the Kaiser."

"Yes, I got that," said Lantier, slightly peeved.

He made a note of the dog's name and, while there was a pause in the interrogations, noticed that the animal had fallen silent again.

"And what happened to 'Wilhelm' in Salonika?"

"You don't have a cigarette, do you?"

This time, the major had anticipated the ploy. He'd armed himself with a pack of shag and some cigarette papers. Morlac busied his fingers rolling. Like all soldiers who'd been in the war, he was good at this. But anyone could tell he was deliberately doing it slowly because the main aim, back there, had been to pass the time.

"Salonika," he said, not looking up from his work, "was a strange place."

He'd made a plump cigarette and was flattening it between fingers blackened by manual labor.

"I've never seen so many different people. French, English, Italian, Greek, Serbian, Senegalese, Annamite, Armenian, Albanian, Turkish . . . "

"But it was mostly the French in command of the expeditionary force, wasn't it?"

"In command! In command of what, that's what I'd like to know. No one spoke the same language. No one knew what he was meant to be doing or where he was meant to be going. And down in the port was worse than anywhere else. In all that mess, a dog had nothing to worry about at all. It was heaven, even. Piles of garbage on the quay, carcasses of every sort of animal rotting in the sun, people sitting on the ground to eat and throwing bones and peelings behind them: He didn't even have to chase rats anymore."

"But you didn't stay in the port?" Lantier asked.

"Well, yes, for a few days, until everything was unloaded by ancient cranes that kept breaking down. The officers fussed around on their horses. Headquarters sent orders and counterorders. Nobody understood a thing."

"Then were you transferred to Salonika itself?"

"And how! They made us parade through the city, with music and flags. We liked it because it was a beautiful place, at least around the center. There were wide avenues with palm trees, and plane trees. But afterwards we had to go through the filthy suburbs, and eventually we were out in the country, marching northwards. The marching raised these hellish clouds of dust that never settled. Mind you, when you go to war in the infantry you have to be prepared to put up with everything."

He looked away as he said this, as if to hide his distress. All at once Lantier felt very close to him. He was assailed by jumbled images of endless marching and exhausting watches, memories of appalling fear, hunger, cold and thirst. During the ensuing silence, he got the impression the other man was shuddering.

"Well, anyway," Morlac concluded, "let's say it was hot."

He took a long drag on his cigarette.

"There was a large camp on the plain to the north of the city. It was well organized but we only passed through. Every time we arrived somewhere we thought it was over, that we'd be setting up camp. But we always set off again and always heading north. The terrain was getting more and more mountainous, the tracks were full of stones, and we had to heave our equipment up through all that. We could see what they were doing: It was going to be the front for us."

"Was the front far from Salonika?"

"What did we know when we set out? Luckily, there were boys coming back down who told us about the fighting. It was only thanks to them that we knew Serbia had given in and was occupied by the Austrians and the Bulgarians, and we were going up there to try to take it back. We found this out by chance, in snatches, and there were plenty of rumors thrown in too. We couldn't tell the truth from the lies. In Salonika we'd heard talk of a spring offensive. We eventually realized it had been delayed and would be starting now. It was going to depend directly on us. That's why everyone already knew what to expect when we were sent to the front line."

The evening meal had arrived. It was prepared at the hospital with the food for the sick, and a nurse's aide delivered four servings in a can to the prison: two for the prisoner and two for Dujeux. The jailer was mortified disturbing the officer, but he felt that a meal was genuinely more important: He liked to eat his food hot and, until the prisoner was served, he had orders not to touch his own meal. Lantier suspended his questioning and left the prison, promising himself he wouldn't make the mistake of arriving so late the following day.

* * *

The major had slept very badly. A group of partygoers had been carousing under his window in the middle of the night and he hadn't managed to get back to sleep afterwards.

He kept thinking about Morlac, about his refusal to grab at the lines he'd thrown him. Why wouldn't he agree to say he'd been drunk? Why not admit he harbored a real passion for his dog and that was why he'd momentarily lost his head? He'd get a light sentence and no one would say any more about it.

All the same, without understanding why, Lantier was grateful to him for not backing down. Since his appointment as a military investigator, he'd seen a lot of straightforward cases: utterly guilty or truly innocent. It wasn't very interesting and, with these cases, he'd put all his energy into making them more complicated, trying to find the element of idealism in a culprit or the darker side of an innocent man.

With Morlac, he felt he was dealing with a more complex defendant, in whom there was a combination of good and bad. It was irritating, appalling even, when he came to think about it. But at least there was a mystery to solve.

He got up before dawn. The ground floor of the hotel was shrouded in darkness but there was light coming through the glazed door to the staff area. Georgette, the hotel's aging cook, was riddling the fire in the stove. She sat him down on the corner of the table covered in chinaware where she was laying out dishes.

"Do you know the village of Vallenay?"

"It's a couple of miles away, on the Saint-Amand road."

"Would someone be able to take me there this morning?"

"What time would you be coming back?"

"For lunch."

"In that case, take the bicycle in the courtyard. Madame

lends it out occasionally to customers who want to visit the area."

When Lantier set off, the sun was sifting through the hedgerows creating a dazzling pincushion of light. Beyond the station he was straight out in the country and there were more signs of life than in town. Carts traveled along the road, harnessed horses were starting work in the fields. He could hear the farm laborers clicking their tongues to keep them moving. Swallows flew in delirious circles through the still-cool sky.

After a long rise, the road dropped down toward a wide plain dotted with ponds. The water flowed from one to the other. In winter they made the area even damper. Willows grew along their banks, and the surrounding fields were striped with the tall stems of bulrushes because they were flooded for six months of the year. But in this oppressive heat, the place was cool, shady, and not as dry as the town.

After asking an old carter for directions, Lantier had no trouble finding the house where Valentine lived. You had to follow a path that ran alongside the last of the ponds. Even in the height of summer, parts of the path dove down into thick, black mud, and you had hop over on stones that had been thrown into it. Lantier hid the bicycle in a thicket of hawthorn and continued on foot.

Valentine was in her vegetable garden, a large square of land she'd been turning over by hand for years now. It had given her gnarled fingers with black-edged nails. She never spoke to anyone without crossing her hands behind her back to hide them.

When she saw the officer coming up the path toward her home, she let go of her basket, stood up and clasped her hands in the small of her back.

Lantier du Grez stopped three paces away from her and doffed his forage cap. In the sunlight his uniform looked worn and felt almost violent, it was so out of place to be dressed like that in such heat. It could only be due to an unpleasant wish to stand out from other people and incarnate a sense of authority. Now that the war was over it was mostly ridiculous.

"You must be . . . Valentine."

The attorney had given a first name. That had been enough to find her but, when it came to addressing her, this ignorance on his part looked like overfamiliarity, and he flushed.

She was a tall, thin girl. For all her simple blue cotton dress, she didn't look like a farmer. Her long bare arms with thick veins streaming down them, her dark hair, which was most likely cut with the same shears she used for the sheep, her bony face—nothing about her suggested bucolic peacefulness but rather the torture nature can subject people to when it is their only means of eking out a subsistence. And yet the insults inflicted by winter and manual labor had not robbed the beauty and nobility from this body they'd afflicted. Embattled on all sides, these qualities had withdrawn into her eyes. Valentine's eyes were black, but shining, direct and clear, not only in the way she looked at Lantier but the way her expression truly opened a pathway to her soul. Despite her destitute appearance, her eyes proclaimed not only that she accepted her situation but also that she was not resigned to it. It was more than pride: It was defiance.

Hearing a man's voice, a child had come out onto the doorstep. With a brusque wave, Valentine told him to disappear. The child took off toward the forest.

"What do you want from me?"

During the four years of war, a visit from a soldier had always signaled death. That had left its mark. Lantier forced a smile and tried to look friendly. He gave her his name and credentials. The words "investigating officer" made the young woman wince.

"What have I . . . "

"Do you know Jacques Morlac?"

She nodded, glancing over to the edge of the woods, as if to check the child was no longer there. The sun was already high in the sky and the heat had invaded the last strongholds of cool air. Lantier could feel the sweat trickling from his armpits.

"Is there somewhere we could talk?"

He wanted to say, "In the shade."

"Come," she said, leading him toward the house.

The door stood wide open. As he stepped in from the sunlight, Lantier took a moment to acclimatize to the darkness inside. He tripped on the irregular floor tiles and steadied himself on the corner of a large sideboard. Valentine offered him a chair, and he sat down with one elbow on the table. She brought over a pitcher of water and a bottle of cordial. The cork was crusty with sugar and Valentine waved aside the flies.

Without being too obvious, Lantier studied the room and was surprised. It wasn't a peasant's home. This was the country, of course: Bunches of dried herbs hung from the ceiling; the shelves beside the chimney breast were full of glass jars, jellies and jams of every sort; cheeses and salted meats gave off their distinctive smell from behind the wire mesh of a larder. But added to these were details that clashed. Firstly, the walls were covered with reproductions.

They were mostly illustrations cut from reviews. The damp had corrugated the paper and the inks had smudged. But there were recognizable masterpieces such as Michelangelo's *David* and *The Battle of San Romano*. There were also less well-known images, faces, nudes, landscapes, and in prominent positions there were even paintings by an avant-garde cubist Lantier couldn't abide.

But more particularly, an entire wall was taken up with books.

The major had a furious longing to get up and go over to look at their spines, to see what they were. From this distance he could already tell they weren't frivolous romances. They mostly had austere dust jackets in drab colors rather than the gaudy covers of mass appeal publications.

Valentine sat down herself and turned all her attention on him. She was smiling but the serious look in her eyes stole all the warmth from her smile. Lantier took a sip of his cordial to gather his composure.

CHAPTER IV

I am conducting an investigation into a soldier who is imprisoned in town, and whom you know."

Valentine understood perfectly but her only reaction was to blink. She was very self-composed.

"His name is Jacques Morlac."

It was rather stupid to name him because they both knew what this was about. The major was irritated with himself for playing this game, and to prove he could cope without it, he skipped a round and went straight to, "How did you meet him?"

"His farm wasn't far from here."

"I thought . . . "

"Yes, by road it's quite a long way. But there's a path that cuts through the ponds and gets you there in ten minutes."

"So you've known him all your life," Lantier stated rather than asking.

"No, because I wasn't born here. I was fifteen when I moved here."

"I've heard your family was decimated by a measles epidemic."

"Only my sister and my mother."

"And your father?"

She looked away and clutched the fabric of her dress in

her lap. Then she lifted her head and looked the officer squarely in the eye again.

"An illness."

"Is measles not an illness?"

"A different one."

He could tell there was an embarrassment, a secret here, but didn't want to push her confidences too far. After all, this was a meeting, not an interrogation. He had nothing to gain from putting her even more on the defensive.

"So you came here after your parents died. Why were you sent here?"

"My parents owned land in the area. And one of my great-aunts lived in this house. She took me in. When she died, two years later, I stayed on alone."

A fragrance hung in the air, not entirely successfully smothering the smell of saltpeter and of a wood fire gone cold. It was an eau de cologne, probably homemade, the sort you might associate with old maids and convents.

"Where did you live with your parents?"

"In Paris."

So that was it. Her misfortune was not to be living meagerly out here in the country, but to have experienced and hoped for another life. She was in exile in this isolated place. The books and reproductions were things she'd managed to save when the ship went down.

"How old were you when you met Morlac?"

"Eighteen."

"And how did you meet him?"

Judging from her reaction, she thought this question intrusive. But she made herself answer it, as she had the others. Lantier got the impression she was a seasoned player at this game, and that her honesty was merely a screen, intended to hide what really mattered.

"I still had livestock at the time, and I needed straw. I went to him to buy some. I guess we . . . liked each other."

"Why didn't you get married?"

"We were waiting for me to come of age. And then the war came along and he left."

"With the dog?"

Valentine burst out laughing. Lantier wouldn't have guessed she could laugh like that, with such abandon and with a fleeting but very visible look of delight on her face. He thought she must love with the same intensity, and found the idea unsettling.

"Yes, with the dog. But what difference does that make?"

"You know what he's been accused of?"

"Oh, that," she shrugged. "He's a hero, isn't he? I don't see why he's being pestered over a trifle."

She said the word "hero" in an unusual way, as if using vocabulary borrowed from a foreign language.

"It's not a trifle," Lantier replied tartly. "It's an outrage to the nation. But, granted, his merits in combat could be taken into account and the slate wiped clean. And that's exactly what I've gone to considerable lengths to suggest to him. But we *would* need him not to be against the idea."

"What do you mean?"

"He needs to apologize, to minimize the incident, to say he was drunk or find some other explanation."

"Is he refusing to?"

"Not only is he refusing but he's aggravating his case with irresponsible comments. You'd think he *wants* to be condemned."

Valentine sat with unseeing eyes and gave a strange smile. Then she jerked her arm abruptly, as if wiping something off the table with the back of her hand. In the process she knocked over the bottle of cordial, which fell to the ground. This unleashed a flurry of activity. She stood up and Lantier did too. She went to fetch a floor cloth from under a cupboard, and gathered up the pieces of glass with a broom. The officer wanted to make himself useful but couldn't think how to. In the end, he let her get on with it and, because he was on his feet, took the opportunity to go and look at the books lined up on the shelves on wall brackets.

He read a few titles at random, on the larger volumes. There were several Zola novels. He also spotted Rousseau's *La Nouvelle Héloïse* and, on another book, although he couldn't be sure, he thought he saw the name Jules Vallès.

"There we are," Valentine said. "I'm so sorry. Everything's fine. Now, what were we saying?"

She was edging him toward the table and seemed particularly keen to get him away from the bookshelves. He went and sat back down and thought at some length before speaking again.

"The fact is," he eventually began, "the case involving Morlac is very likely one of the last I will handle. I'm planning to leave the army and go into civilian life. I'd like to end on an uplifting note, to have good memories of my position, so to speak. If I could succeed in stopping this defendant from going to his death, it would give me tremendous satisfaction and I could leave less heavyhearted. As you can see, it's very selfish."

He was ashamed to admit he had a personal interest in the case. But she'd already more than grasped the fact.

"Morlac is indeed a hero," he went on. "We owe our victory to men like him. I'd like to save him. But that can only be done against his will, because he's determined to be condemned to death, and I don't understand why. That's why I'm here."

She looked at him steadily, unblinking, waiting to hear what would come next.

"Could I ask you a rather prying question but one I believe to be of key importance?"

She didn't reply and, as she'd expected, he didn't wait for an answer.

"Is your child his?"

She knew he would come to this.

"Jules is his son."

"For him to be three years old, he must have been conceived . . . during the war."

"Jacques came home on leave and, while he was here, we made love almost continuously."

Lantier felt himself flushing but he was too driven by the subject to falter at this obstacle of propriety.

"Has he recognized him as such on the local register?"

"No."

"He could have done."

"Yes."

"But he didn't."

"No."

Lantier sprang to his feet and walked to the door. He hovered on the doorstep for a moment, his eyes wide and scorched by the sun. The child was back. It was a little boy dressed in mud-colored scraps of cloth stitched together. He'd caught a mole and was prodding it with a stick, without any spite but without any mercy either.

"Have you seen him since he came back?" Lantier asked.

"No."

"But he came back here for you."

"I don't think so. If he came home, it must be for his farm."

"Except he hasn't set foot on the place. He was lodging in a furnished room in town."

This was one of the pieces of information that featured in the policemen's report. Morlac's land had been farmed by his brother-in-law since his sister's marriage. Morlac hadn't even been to see them when he returned. He'd moved into a family-run boardinghouse under a false name, but the woman running the place had recognized him immediately. She'd put this anomaly down to the traumas of war.

"I didn't know that," Valentine said.

"Did he try to see his son?"

"Not that I know."

"Would you allow him to?"

"Of course."

"Would you permit me to tell him that?"

She shrugged her shoulders.

"Are you going to visit him in prison?"

"I've no idea."

It was clear she'd been considering this for a long time. Something was holding her back, and Lantier didn't have the heart to ask her what.

As he pedaled back on his bike, the sun beat down on him mercilessly. He watched the front wheel wobbling under the effects of tiredness and the heat.

And was annoyed he hadn't asked more questions.

* * *

The abbey-church clock was striking two when Lantier put the bicycle back into the hotel's yard. He went up to his room for a quick wash and to change his shirt. Then he headed for the dining room where Georgette had left his lunch on a table. On a plate covered with a white cloth he found a burbot tail and pureed oyster plant. Two rashly consumed glasses of Bordeaux forced him back upstairs for a half-hour siesta.

It was almost half past three when he set off for the prison. The heat had dropped slightly. It was now colored by the hint of an easterly wind bringing in cooler air and smells from the forest. There were times, like this, when Lantier already felt very close to civilian life, and he was gripped by anticipatory nostalgia for the military. He thought he would miss it. He derived genuine physical pleasure from walking through this town strapped into the uniform he would soon stop wearing.

As he turned onto Rue Danton, he walked out into the glaring sun on the square facing the prison. He almost tripped over a body lying across the sidewalk. It was Wilhelm, Morlac's dog. He was lying on one side with his tongue lolling right out, almost down to the street. He looked exhausted by the days and nights spent howling. His eyes were bright with fever, and sunken in their sockets. He must have been appallingly thirsty. Lantier went over to a fountain in the shade of a linden tree in one corner of the square. He grasped the crank and worked the pump. Hearing running water, the dog clambered to his feet and came over to the fountain.

His tongue worked methodically as he drank while Lantier continued turning the small creaking bronze handle.

When the dog had slaked his thirst, the major sat down on a bench by the fountain, in the same patch of shade. He wondered whether Wilhelm would go back onto the square and start barking again. But instead the animal stood steadfastly by the bench with his eyes pinned on the major.

Close up, the dog was a painful sight. He really looked like an old warrior. Several scars on his back and sides were evidence of wounds from gunshots or shrapnel. It looked as if they hadn't been tended to, and the flesh had managed to knit together as best it could by forming ridges, hardened patches and calluses. One of the dog's hind legs was deformed and when he sat down, he had to lay it at a diagonal to avoid falling over on his side. Lantier reached out a hand and the dog moved closer to be stroked. His head was uneven to the touch, as if he were wearing a dented helmet. The right-hand side of his muzzle was pale pink and smooth of hair, the result of a severe burn. But in the middle of this ravaged face shone two eyes full of pathos. Wilhelm stood motionless while he was stroked. He gave the impression he'd been trained not to fuss, to make as little noise as possible, except to raise the alert. But his eyes alone expressed everything that other dogs display with their tails and paws, by whining or rolling on the ground.

Lantier watched the way this old dog wrinkled his forehead and tilted his head slightly, opening his eyes wide to express contentment or narrowing them slyly to question what the person he was with might want or intend to do.

These facial expressions, teamed with eloquent little movements of his neck, allowed him to cover the whole gamut of emotions. Showing his feelings but, more significantly, responding to those of others.

Sitting there on that bench, maddened by the heat, the investigating officer felt a terrible weariness build inside him. Four years serving his country fighting, and two defending order and authority by sentencing poor devils to death had worn him out. Moments ago he'd already been feeling nostalgia for military life; right now he was closer to regretting the emptiness it had left him with. Would he ever be able to do anything else?

The dog must have sensed his despondency. He had moved closer and had laid his muzzle on Lantier's knee. His breathing had slowed. It sounded painful.

Lantier was still stroking him. His hand smoothed affectionately over the animal's muscular neck; he scratched Wilhelm's ears and the dog shook his head with pleasure.

The major had had a dog himself once. He was called Corgan, and Lantier remembered how he would pet him for ages, on the steps to his parents' house in the Perche region. Corgan was a pedigree dog, a black-and-white Pointer, well fed and looked after in his case. But he'd had the same devotedness, and Hugues Lantier had had an opportunity to gauge this the year he turned thirteen.

In those days the Lantiers used to spend the summer at their estate on the banks of the Huisne, and would head back to Paris toward October. Only Hugues's father couldn't be away such a long time. He was senior banking executive for a bank based on the Rue Lafitte, and would return to Paris in early August. Hugues stayed on at the country estate with his two younger sisters and his mother.

The family was starting to experience financial difficulties and would soon be forced to sell this property, which had been inherited from an uncle. In the meantime, they had reduced their staff to a cook and an aging retainer who used to go off in his cart to buy provisions.

One autumn day burglars got into the house at nightfall, simply by climbing the boundary wall which had almost crumbled away in places. They were a gang of opportunists afraid of nothing and no one, and never stayed in the same place long. There were three of them and they took orders from a leader, a tall blond fellow with a bushy beard.

They burst into the living room just before the evening meal. The leader whooped as he herded Hugues's mother and her two daughters into a corner of the room. His accomplices brought in the cook and the old servant, and pushed them into the same corner. The third man tied them up with a washing line, and lined them up side by side on the floor behind the piano. Only Hugues had escaped because he'd been playing in his bedroom on the second floor when they arrived. He watched the scene between two balusters on the galleried landing.

What happened next was very violent and very messy. The thieves broke into cupboards, emptied wine bottles and feasted on what they found in the larder. Two of them had a fight, hurling ornaments and paintings at each other. It was an extraordinary sight for the child. In a matter of minutes, the peaceful order in the house was obliterated and replaced by unbridled primitive desires and senseless violence. Hugues waited for the nightmare to end.

Later, well into the night, one of the pillagers who was less befuddled by their blowout realized that they had four women at their disposal and could derive some pleasure from them. Hugues's sisters were only ten and eleven, but the thug didn't let a detail like that trouble him. He walked behind the piano, laughing loudly, studied the bodies lying there, and dragged one of them into the middle of the living room. It was Solange, the elder of the two little girls, wearing a blue dress with an overly full skirt that gave her womanly curves. The drunk made her stand up and introduced her to the others who were slumped on armchairs. The poor child was terrified. Hugues could see her face, her eyes wide with terror. His first instinct was to come out of hiding to help his sister. But that would only have handed over yet another victim to the gang, who already had five at their mercy. He waited, eyes closed.

A piercing scream made him open them again. Solange, whose dress had been ripped off by her attacker, was shrieking with all her might. Surprised by this scream, the brigand stepped back. At that exact moment, something launched across the room and leapt onto him. It was Corgan. The man fell backward and struggled to break free, bellowing hoarsely. The dog had grabbed him by the neck and was pinning his prey to the floor, devouring his face. The others were paralyzed with fear, frozen in contemplation of the scene. They soon gathered their wits and got to their feet. The dog let go of his first victim, who was howling in pain, and squared up to them.

Making the most of the confusion, Hugues came down the stairs, hidden by the banisters. When he reached the hall he opened the glazed door that led into the garden, and fled. The moon had risen and lit up the countryside.

He had no trouble finding his way. The village was about half a mile away, as you came out of the woods. He woke the local policeman, who raised the alarm. Ten armed men were soon setting off toward the house. They came across the bandits loading as much food and wine as they could onto the cart. They were fodder for the penal colonies.

But Corgan was dead.

Lantier had never forgotten this dog's sacrifice, but he rarely thought about it. Morlac's case had made it resurface in his mind. And now he thought of it, he felt this dramatic event had not been without consequence in his life. He had joined the army to defend order against barbarity. He had become a soldier to serve mankind. Which was a misunderstanding, of course. It wasn't long before war came along and showed him that the opposite was true, that order feeds off human beings, it consumes them and crushes them. But deep down and in spite of everything, he was still bound to his vocation. And that vocation had its origins in the actions of a dog.

He must have fallen asleep. True, he'd cut short his siesta at the hotel in order to get back to the prison sooner. And now here he was dreaming again as he sat on this bench, stroking the dog.

Wilhelm still had his muzzle on Lantier's knee. He was looking at him, swiveling his eyes in a comical way. Lantier gently drew back his leg and pushed the dog aside. Then he stood up and stretched. He straightened his uniform and headed for the prison. The sun had moved round, the square was almost entirely in the shade.

He knocked at the door, and Dujeux opened up for him. As he stepped inside he heard the dog start barking again in the distance.

CHAPTER V

It must have been Morlac's day for a shower. He was clean and freshly shaven, his hair was combed and he smelled of Marseille soap. The interlude with the dog had put Lantier in a good mood. When he arrived in the cell he sat in his usual place and opened the file.

"Where were we? Ah, yes! Salonika."

"Do you really want me to talk about all this?"

"Not all of it. Just the essentials."

"Well, so we reached the front."

"What did the front consist of in that part of the world?"

Morlac was scraping under one of his nails with a beveled stick. Now that he was clean, he'd set about scouring every inch of himself.

"Valleys surrounded by sort of rounded mountains. There weren't really any trenches, not facing each other like in Picardie or the Somme. The enemy positions were quite a way off. We hid in holes and we often moved around. The artillery fired blindly."

"Any mud?"

"Not too much. But it was hot in summer and freezing in winter. Unbelievable differences in temperature. The hardest thing was definitely that we spent long stretches of time on the front line. The Oriental Force was always short of men. No troops came to relieve us. We were so, so bored, weeks on end like that."

"What did you do?"

"Well, I read."

"Did the others?"

"Not so much."

Lantier made up his mind to ask some questions he hadn't clearly formulated the previous day, when he'd seen him reading Victor Hugo.

"And how is it that you could read? You left school very young, from what I think I know."

Morlac muttered to himself.

"I like reading, there's no harm in that," he said.

"You must have acquired this taste for reading from someone?"

The prisoner shrugged. "Possibly."

Lantier decided the moment had come. He put down his notes and stood up. He took a couple of steps toward the far wall which was covered in obscene graffiti. Then he spun round and said, "I went to visit you wife this morning. You don't seem to be in a hurry to get back to her. But I do think she's waiting for you."

"She's not my wife."

"But she's the mother of your child."

Morlac's eyes suddenly flashed with hate.

"Mind your own business! Anyway, that's enough of this interrogating. Sentence me to death and be done with it."

"In that case," Lantier replied, "let's get back to your dog, because this is about him."

He was briefly tempted to describe his moment alone with Wilhelm, on the bench. But he was keen to maintain his authority as an investigating officer, and this anecdote ran the risk of looking like familiarity. His curt tone of voice and the way he'd buried himself in his notes had their effect on Morlac, who dropped his head, like a reprimanded schoolboy.

"After more than a month at the front and in the surrounding area," he carried on automatically, "we were evacuated to Monastir. It was the end of the spring offensive. Wilhelm couldn't come with us because he had an injury in his side from a shell blast."

"Did you leave him at the front?"

"The guy who took over my blockhouse agreed to look after him. He was a Serb, evacuated to Corfu after the defeat in Belgrade. He had a funny way of looking at Wilhelm. I got the feeling he'd eaten quite a lot of dogs during the retreat. All I asked was that he bury him if he did die."

"But he didn't die."

"No, he's a tough nut, that dog. When he was pretty much healed he made the journey on his own, through the Vardar gorges to Monastir. He was hit about the head with sticks, and when he arrived his eyes were almost closed from all the blood that had trickled into them."

"Then what?"

"We spent the winter in a billet and that's what saved us. The cold there is incredible. Apart from the mountain infantry boys, no one had seen temperatures like it. When we were sent back to the front in March, there were still seven-foot snowdrifts along the side of the road."

"And the dog was still going strong?"

"He got his strength back in Monastir. I didn't take much care of him. But there was an English fusilier, I used to play cards with him in the evenings, and he really took to him. You know what the English are like with animals.

He'd bring him stuff to eat, leftover rations, not scraps. And he even found some disinfectant for the wounds on his back."

"Wasn't the dog tempted to stay with the Englishman?" Lantier asked with genuine interest. "I don't mean to be judgmental, but you don't seemed to have given him much affection, this dog of yours."

"I've told you. That's the way I am. But I was his master and he knew that."

"All in all, he stayed with you for the whole of the war."

"Yes."

"Did you have much fighting on that front?"

"Not really. It was a strange war, with very little contact. One time we bumped into an Austrian patrol by chance. We had to use our bayonets to get out of that. It was the first time I saw Wilhelm in action. He understood who were the enemies and attacked the Austrians, he got it right every time."

"You didn't get a mention for that combat."

"There was no reason to," Morlac said dismissively. "There was nothing glorious about it. We saved our own skins, that's all. And Fritz could only think of one thing, and that was getting away, too."

"What did you do the rest of the time?"

"Routine things: patrols, guard duties, a bit of reconnaissance. But most of all we were sick. It's a very bad climate. I avoided malaria but I got terrible dysentery. As you seem interested in the dog, I can tell you he watched over me the whole time I was ill and went to find help every time I needed something."

Now that Lantier knew Wilhelm a little, he was very touched by this devotion he'd shown during the war. But it only made his master's coldness all the more surprising. The fact that, like all country folk, Morlac had had a utilitarian relationship with animals, deprived of any effusive emotion—that Lantier could understand. But there seemed to be something else, some sort of resentment. What had happened between them that the prisoner wasn't saying?

The investigator dug deeper.

"Did Wilhelm take part in the fighting that earned you the mention?" he asked.

Morlac had taken four or five drags on his cigarette in succession. Smoking had a visibly relaxing effect on him. He leaned back until his head touched the wall. He stayed in that position for a long time and then sat up again abruptly and looked at Lantier.

"It's a long story, sir. We'd be more comfortable going through it outside, don't you think? Couldn't we go out for a walk?"

Lantier wasn't far from having the same idea himself. He'd almost had enough of this dark cell with its stuffy tobacco smell when the weather outside was so beautiful. He was reaching the decisive part of Morlac's story, and wanted to secure the man's trust.

"You're right. We could walk around the yard."

It wasn't the appointed time but there were, after all, no other prisoners and Dujeux could perfectly well open up the space used as an exercise yard. The major went to find the guard who came over all important and thought about it at length in silence, considering whether such a request was compatible with the regulations. Lantier ended up making the decision for him by telling him it was an order.

The jailer grumbled to himself as he turned the key in

76 - JEAN-CHRISTOPHE RUFIN

the lock, and the two men went out into an area the size of a tennis court. Grass and mounds of moss between the paving stones were yellowing under the effects of the mid-summer heat. They would have the whole rest of the year to soak up moisture. The surrounding walls were of rough-hewn stone and the thick pointing in crumbling cement gave the whole thing a medieval look. Over this charmless, ageless courtyard hung the canopy of an indigo sky with small, orangey clouds drifting slowly overhead. The top of a larch appeared above the wall.

Morlac looked very happy to be breathing in the open air. Lantier got the impression that his imprisonment didn't trouble him so long as he could see the sky.

They cut diagonally across the yard, then started strolling around the outside, as prisoners do the world over.

"I don't want there to be any misunderstanding," Morlac said, "as a result of this report you're writing. That's why there's something I have to say right away: You're wrong about the mention I received."

"What do you mean?"

"Well, so, if you'll forgive the expression, you're beating about the bush. You keep asking me questions about my dog. You're trying to get me to say I love him, that he's my comrade-in-arms. I can see where you want this to go."

"It's in your interest, I've already said that."

Morlac had stopped in his tracks and turned to face the officer. He'd reverted to his solemn, stubborn expression. The fresh air certainly hadn't had an effect on him for long.

"I don't want you to find attenuating circumstances for me."

"Don't you want to get out of here?"

"I don't want what I did to be misrepresented. You won't hush up what I have to say."

"Well, this is your opportunity to explain yourself clearly. Because I'll readily admit I don't understand what you did, nor your determination to be heavily penalized."

Morlac didn't seem concerned by this admission. He started walking again.

"Do you remember what happened in 1917, sir?"

Lantier glanced at him anxiously. 1917, the darkest year of the war; the year of the disastrous Nivelle Offensive at the Chemin des Dames, and of widespread mutinies; the year of despair and contradictory upheavals; the Americans arriving and the Russians retreating; the defeat of the Italians and Clemenceau's accession to power. This was not looking good.

Luckily, Dujeux was standing by the door jangling his keys. The excursion into the yard hadn't altered the rest of the routine, and it was food time. For once, Lantier was pleased with himself for starting the questioning so late. They'd have plenty of time the next day to embark on what promised to be no pleasure ride for the officer.

* * *

On his way back to the hotel, Lantier thought about making a detour to go and pet the dog. It grieved him to see the animal barking again, utterly exhausted, propped against a stone post at the far end of Place Michelet.

But it was late afternoon and people were coming back outside. A cart was heading up the hill from the abbey-church, creaking over the paving stones. A laborer in a black jacket whistled on his way with a ladder on his shoulder.

Lantier didn't want to run the risk of spawning rumors in town about his sentimentality, his compassion for animals. He crossed the square in a dignified manner and set off along the Rue du 4-Septembre.

A little further on he went into La Civette to buy some tobacco. This was in anticipation of the next day's interrogation. He smoked little himself, but Morlac had taken to asking him for cigarettes, and he was keen to have this card in his hand for the round they were about to play.

As he came out of the smoke shop, he met the squad commander of the local police force. He'd been wanting to meet him since he arrived but had been told the man was away.

"Squadron Sergeant-Major Gabarre," the policeman announced in a gravelly voice, standing to attention.

Short and ruddy-faced with a protruding stomach, he was every inch the country bumpkin. He must have been born to farming but joined the force because an opportunity arose. That decision probably derived from the same pragmatic reasoning that made a peasant sow his field with lucerne rather than oats, depending on what the market was doing. From what Lantier had gathered in his conversations with the only other policeman (because the squad in this quiet town comprised all of two men), Gabarre had spent his entire career here.

"I've just returned from a funeral twenty miles away, sir. I'm so sorry I wasn't here to help with your inquiries."

The police officer couldn't have served in the war. He was quaking at the sight of this major and hadn't acquired the ironic aloofness with which regular soldiers now tempered their demonstrations of obedience.

"At ease, sergeant. Everything is going perfectly well, thank you kindly. Do you have a moment?"

"I'm at your disposal, sir."

"In that case, come with me to the Place Étienne-Dolet, I think that's the name of the little square over there, where there are chairs under the trees."

They walked over together in silence. The policeman had a slight limp. It was more likely gout than a war wound. When they reached the square they sat down on a couple of chairs around a small enameled table. Gabarre put his kepi on his knee, fiddling nervously with its shiny visor. The waiter came to take their order and brought out two glasses of beer.

The streets were steeped in the beginnings of purplish shadow although the sky was still light, striped with pink clouds. The air was cool and all the damp of months of rain seeped from the walls. But the chairs and the ground were still warm and lent this part of the evening a sensuality that was all the more precious because it was so obviously fleeting.

"I've been to the prison every day. My interrogation of the accused is almost over."

The police officer took this statement as a reproach.

"I'm sorry," he said.

But Lantier couldn't see how the other man's absence had inconvenienced him, and reassured him it hadn't.

"Did you know him, this Morlac, before he stirred up this commotion?"

"By sight, like anyone else," Gabarre said and then added knowingly, "strange fellow."

"In what way strange?"

"I couldn't put it into words, sir. He was someone you never really saw. He had no friends, no family. When he came home from war, the mayor arranged a ceremony for the troops. He came, sat alone in his corner, drinking, and then left without saying anything to anyone. The town clerk was convinced he'd made off with some silver cutlery. They thought about carrying out a search. In the end, bearing in mind his services to the country at the front, they abandoned the idea. But he did it almost openly, as if he already wanted to create a scandal then."

"Do you know Valentine, the mother of his child?"

Gabarre had relaxed slightly. He'd finished his glass of beer, and the major gestured to the waiter to bring another.

"She's a whole other story. We have an eye on her."

"I thought she never left her house. I went to see her. She lives practically in the middle of the woods."

"She doesn't go out but there are people who pay her visits."

"What sort of people?"

The police officer leaned forward and glanced around warily.

"Workmen, people on the run," he slipped the words out in a muffled voice. "She thinks we don't know. That's deliberate, to keep them coming. But we're actually watching them, and when they leave her we pounce on them."

He gave a sly smile like a poacher revealing where he's set his traps.

"Do you know her family?" he asked Lantier, sure of the effect this would have.

As he expected, Lantier looked surprised.

"I thought she had no family left. They all died of disease. She told me so herself."

"They may well be dead, but they once lived," countered Gabarre, proud of his logic.

"I'm perfectly prepared to believe that. And so?"

"So she didn't tell you who her father was."

"No."

"She doesn't brag about it. You see, her father was a German Jew, on close terms with that Rosa Luxembourg who was assassinated in Berlin last winter. He was a member of the Workers' International. He was an agitator and a rabid pacifist. He was arrested and died in prison in Angers. Apparently he had TB."

"And her mother?"

"She was a local girl. Her parents sent her to Paris to train as a seamstress in one of the large stores. That's where she met the émigré. She fell madly in love with him and they were married. She came from a good family, mind you, livestock merchants who owned land in the area. She inherited a small share of it but most of it went to her brothers. Luckily for her, that was after her husband had died, because he would have made her sell the lot to raise money for the cause."

With the second glass of beer, the police sergeant had completely relaxed. Lantier was surprised to find him so sprightly of mind and so well informed. He'd guessed he might be playing his cards close to his chest, but not to this extent.

"The poor woman never benefited from her inheritance," Gabarre went on. "She was taken just after by an epidemic, and her older daughter along with her. All that was left was this Valentine who apparently looks exactly like her father, and is just as fanatical as he was."

"She doesn't look it, though."

But as he said this, Lantier suddenly remembered the girl's hard eyes and the way she talked about the war.

"She's crafty, that one. She was taken in by an aunt of

her mother's, a half-feral creature who'd set up home in that back of beyond place so she didn't have to see anyone. She must have taught her her witch's spells."

"Do you know why Morlac didn't go back to her after the war?"

The police officer shrugged.

"Can anyone work out what people like that are thinking? They probably had a fight."

"Did she meet someone else?"

"Like I said, plenty of people go through there. The revolutionaries use her house as a hideout for guys who're in trouble with the police. As for knowing whether she had something going with one of them, I couldn't tell you."

It was now completely dark. The waiter had lit oil lamps around the tables, and two gas lamps, one on either side of the square, cast a mauve light on the paving stones. Lantier looked at his watch. It was time he went back to the hotel, if he hoped to find some supper there.

"Would you like to make yourself useful, sergeant?"

Gabarre suddenly remembered who he was talking to. He sat up and said a loud, "Yes, sir."

"Right, well, try to find out whether Morlac has seen his son since he's been home."

"It won't be very easy, but . . . "

"I'm counting on you. Come and see me when you can, if you find anything."

Lantier left a few coins on the table and stood up. The police sergeant wanted to give him a military salute, but the major shook his hand.

As he walked back to the hotel, he thought he heard the dog's barking carried on the wind from time to time. But it was weak and very irregular.

CHAPTER VI

V alentine didn't want to go inside. She was standing by the door to the hotel. Although he was of no use to anyone before he'd had his coffee, Lantier had no trouble recognizing her. He wasn't expecting her to visit, at least not so soon and not so early in the morning. But she must have been thinking all night, not had a moment's sleep, and now here she was, her face unreadable, her mind made up.

"Good morning, Valentine," he said, coming out onto the doorstep. "Come in and have some coffee."

She was carrying a basket with both hands, holding it at arm's length, with an embarrassed expression. Lantier thought of her father, the political agitator, whom Gabarre said she resembled. He was most likely the same sort of character, capable of setting fire to a bourgeois house but intimidated by an invitation to enter one. In the end he persuaded her and she went inside.

As he followed her along the hotel's corridors, with their painted wallpaper and pictures on the walls, he grasped what held her back. At home, she was in keeping with her surroundings. Here, her coarse dress and wooden clogs made her look like a slattern.

He showed her to the back of the building, onto a small terrace where there were some garden chairs. She was less out of place in this outdoor setting than in the lounges with their decorative moldings.

He ordered a coffee. She didn't want anything. This refusal seemed to demonstrate a determination not to accept anything from anyone she considered her enemy. Had it been more moderate, this principle might have seemed respectable and even formidable. Pushed to extremes and applied to the most insignificant things, such as a cup of coffee, there was something laughable and puerile about it.

She'd put her basket on the ground and was pretending to rifle through it, just to have something to do. When the serving girl had brought Lantier's coffee and they were left alone, she glowered at Lantier and, with no preamble, cut straight to, "Actually, I do want to see him. And I want him to know."

"I've suggested it to him but . . . "

"That's for sure, he'll say no. But you mustn't just 'suggest' it."

She imitated the fluty way Lantier had said the word. This intonation alone was a gauge of the violent feelings that gripped her at the thought of the army.

"What exactly would you like me to say to him?"

"That I *have* to see him. It has to happen. And I want to."

"Leave it with me. I'll come to your house to bring you the answer myself if he changes his mind."

"That won't be necessary."

"Why not?"

"I'll stay in town in the meantime."

Lantier showed his surprise with one raised eyebrow.

"There's a woman I know who sells vegetables next to me in the market. She'll put me up for as long as it takes. She lives behind the covered market."

"Very well."

"Is he allowed letters?"

"Yes, but the jailer opens them and reads them."

"In that case, I'd rather speak," she hissed.

She had risen to her feet and picked up her basket, resting it on her hip like a lavender girl.

"Tell him that when he came back he got things wrong. The man was a comrade."

"Do you mean that he . . . "

"It's not you I'm talking to, but him. And him alone."

She was clearly distressed and her emotion sat awkwardly with the restraint she imposed on herself. She was better off slipping away. She barely said goodbye to Lantier, and he made no effort to keep her there.

* * *

When he arrived at the prison to take Morlac's final confession, the investigating officer was surprised by the silence in the square. There was no sign of Wilhelm and he couldn't be heard. Lantier asked Dujeux what had happened to the dog.

"He was at the end of his tether from all that barking. He eventually stopped during the night. In the moonlight I could make him out lying flat out over there. I thought he'd died. To be absolutely honest, I wouldn't have minded. But the nursing assistant told me what had happened when she brought our food."

"Where is he? You know I need that dog for my investigation. He's a contributory factor in the offense, a sort of accomplice or an exhibit."

"He's over there, in one of the houses. You see the little

street that leads off at an angle from the square? It's there, on the ground floor. The first door."

"Have you been in there?"

"I'm not allowed to leave my post."

"True. In that case, I shall go myself."

As he cut across the square, Lantier wondered why he'd invented the story about an exhibit. Morlac could easily be judged at a court-martial without producing the dog. It was all in the policemen's statement, and his own report of his investigation would complement that. The truth was far more stupid. He wanted to see the dog. He took a personal interest in what happened to him. This thought made him smile, but he still didn't turn back.

The house Dujeux had pointed out was a one-story cottage shoehorned between two buildings. It was a vestige of what had once been a neighborhood of simple hovels, when the town wasn't much more than a village made up of a row of little single-story houses. There was a stone frame around the door. Clumsily engraved on the lintel and now nearly worn away was the date 1778.

Lantier rapped the bronze knocker, which was shaped like a hand. A woman's voice called from inside straightaway, telling him to come in. He stepped into a dark hallway that opened onto a tiny living room. The mustiness of rotting carpets mingled with a smell of cold cooking fat encrusted in the curtains and the fabric covering the armchairs. In this poky place, the height of summer was merely a digression, soon forgotten. In normal weather, in other words all year round, the stale air would never be replaced. It was doubtful whether the windows still opened.

There was so much furniture it was only just possible to

move. An oval pedestal table stood in the center of the room. Between this and the marble fireplace with its cracked mantelpiece, they'd managed to squeeze an overly large sofa. Wilhelm was lying there on a sheet that had been hastily thrown over it to protect the embroidery.

Against that pale pink background he really did look in bad shape. In the bright light on the square Lantier hadn't fully assessed how thin the animal was. His ribs stood out, his stomach was hollow, and he made a whistling sound from deep inside with every breath. His dull, worn coat left his scars plain to see. He blinked slowly, exhausted, and didn't even move his head when the major came over to pet him.

"Look at the state he's got himself into! Poor creature . . . " said an old woman, holding onto the furniture as she came over. She was wearing a wig which she didn't bother to secure so it slid over to one side like a beret.

"I've fed him every night. Other neighbors took him water to drink. But with this heat, barking like that non-stop, it's killed him."

Lantier nodded. He sat on the edge of the sofa and stroked the dog's neck as he had out on the square. Wilhelm closed his eyes, and his breathing slowed.

"You're the veterinarian then, are you? Mister Paul must have called you. He said he would."

"No. I'm not a veterinarian, unfortunately."

He was afraid she would ask what he was doing there but she was heading back to the kitchen, carrying on with her previous train of thought: "Mind you, he doesn't need a veterinarian. We all know what the poor creature needs. Some shade, some food and some water. That's all."

"Are you going to keep him here?"

"So long as he wants to stay, yes. But when he's better I'll bet he'll go and howl outside the prison again, if they haven't freed his master."

She was coming back into the room carrying a sort of pitcher in cracked enamel.

"Those military bastards!" she grumbled.

Lantier gave a start. Was she speaking to him? How should he reply? When he saw her at closer quarters, though, he understood. She was holding onto the furniture to guide her because she was almost blind. One of her eyes was veiled by a whitish cloud, and the other peered permanently upwards. She definitely wouldn't have noticed his uniform.

"Do you know his master?" he asked.

"Everyone knows him. He's a local boy."

"What's he done wrong?"

Lantier was fascinated to find someone who didn't know who he was, who would speak to him without having to stick to an official version.

"Nothing. He's only ever done good. He just told those butchers a few home truths. They obviously didn't like it and they're taking their revenge."

"The military?"

"Of course, the whole lot of them. The generals, the politicians they serve and the ones who sell the cannons. All the people who sent our local boys to their deaths."

The old woman automatically turned her gaze toward a dresser that stood along one side of the room, between the window and the wall to the hallway. Three framed photographs had been placed there, the faces of three young boys with calm, inane expressions full of hope. The eldest couldn't have been more than twenty-five. Beside them, in a larger frame, a crinkled photograph featured a man standing full-length, all done up in an engineer's uniform.

"My son and my three grandsons," said the old woman, as if she could tell Lantier had turned to look at the pictures.

"All . . ."

"Yes. And in the same year. 1915."

There was a brief silence, then the woman shuddered slightly to brush aside the emotion. She drove a rubber tube into Wilhelm's mouth and lifted up the pitcher to pour the water. The dog swallowed noisily. He coughed and choked but let her carry on, as if he understood it was all for his own good.

"And what would you do if they sentenced his master to death? Could you keep the dog here?"

"Sentenced him to death! Oh, poor miserable soul! I should hope the good Lord won't let a thing like that happen. For four years they came looking for our boys to kill them, but the war's over now. What about the prefect and the police and all the big-shot draft dodgers who did well out of it? It's about time they paid their dues. If they sentenced that boy to death it would be a terrible thing."

The dog had a violent bout of coughing, and water spilled from his mouth, spreading over the sheet.

"Blast! I poured a bit too quickly. Easy, my beauty! Easy!"

She lowered the pitcher and withdrew the tube. All of a sudden a thought came to her, and turning her dead eyes to Lantier, she asked, "Anyway, who are you exactly?"

He felt uncomfortable.

"A friend."

"Of the dog's?" she sniggered.

"Of his master's."

Afraid she would pursue this and he would have to lie, which could have regrettable consequences, he swiftly took his leave.

"I must go, I'm so sorry. I'll come by again. Take good care of him. And thank you. Thank you again."

The major left and as he closed the door he heard the old woman joking with dog:

"He has some funny friends, that master of yours!"

* * *

Lantier hadn't wasted too much time with this detour to the old woman's house. When he reached the prison the abbey-church clock was just striking nine.

He could tell at first glance that Morlac had been waiting for him. A radical change had taken place in the prisoner. He was no longer enduring the major's interrogation, but looking forward to it.

One of the charms of the military is that once an order has been given, it takes another order to abolish it. Lantier had said nothing to the contrary to Dujeux the day before, so the jailer led the defendant and his judge directly out to the courtyard at the back of the building, and closed the door to leave them to talk. From time to time he put his nose up to the square window in the door and came away reassured.

This time Morlac steered the officer toward a stone bench which, happily, was in full sunlight.

"I warn you, this is going to take quite a long time today."

"I've plenty of time."

The cool of the night stayed trapped in the confined space of that courtyard as it would in the bottom of a well, and the sunlight that reached them was like a warm caress.

"I've told you about 1916," said Morlac, "the year I arrived on the eastern front. A year of pointless suffering. Failed offensives, and that winter coming in on top of everything else, freezing up in those mountains, and the bickering between all the different people who made up the Oriental Force. We could call them Allies 'til we were blue in the face, it didn't fool anyone. They each had their own aims. With the English it was about the gateway to India. They did as little as possible in Salonika and, if we'd listened to them, we'd have sent everyone to Egypt. The Italians were only interested in Albania. The Greeks kept changing their minds, some wanted to support the Germans, and some were in favor of the Allies. Basically, it was a shambles at top-brass level. It was even worse for the troops. In winter we froze, and in summer there was malaria and our failing stomachs."

"Did you have any leave?"

Morlac didn't appear to like the question. He looked away.

"No. And I didn't want any, anyway," he said and then quickly changed the subject, going back to his account: "In '17 things got going again with offensives in the north. I was in the eastern sector, in Macedonia. We were up against the Bulgarians. All we knew was Romania had caved in. We had no idea about anything else. The terrain was all gorges and strings of mountains, with ridges where they shot at us from. Our objective was the river Tcherna. But the enemy were well-fortified, and in the end we got dug in, too."

"In fact, it must have been like in France: trenches and pillboxes."

"Waiting, mostly. And we were a long way from home. We didn't get any mail. We went through these strange villages with white houses, they didn't look like anything we'd ever known. You couldn't trust anyone. No one liked us but, God knows, the locals made a song and dance when they saw us. You'd have thought we were the answer to all their prayers, every time. And then two days later we realized they were informing the enemy, and that's when they weren't slitting our throats themselves."

"Were there other Allied troops with you?"

"I'm just coming to that."

Dujeux's face was briefly framed in the small window in the door.

"We had the Annamites to our left. The poor things were freezing to death. They packed it in completely in those conditions. They turned grey and stopped moving. It was hard to get three words out of them."

"It was the same in Argonne."

"My friends told me to keep an eye on Wilhelm because they had a reputation for eating dogs. But he went to their sector two or three times and they didn't do him any harm."

"A lot of exaggerating goes on about that. I never saw them eat dogs."

Morlac gave an evasive shrug. He wanted to get to the point.

"To our right were the Russians. They were so close that our lines met. If we walked along our trenches we came across theirs. They were a friendly bunch and they knew all about winter. They didn't have much to eat but their supply corps always made sure they had something to drink. They made music in the evenings and Wilhelm often went over there. One time they even made him drink some vodka and everyone laughed when he came back because he couldn't walk straight."

The sun had moved round and they shifted to the end of the bench to stay in the light.

"I often went to look for him in the Russian sector, in fact I ended up getting to know quite a few of those boys. There was one, Afoninov, who spoke French and I liked talking with him. He was a regular soldier but he'd had an education. He was a typographer in Saint Petersburg. He'd had some trouble with the Tsar's police, and had been sent to the front without anyone asking his opinion."

"Did the officers keep an eye on him?"

"There weren't many. And I got the feeling all the Russians in that part of the world must have been pretty much like him. They held meetings together and talked politics for hours. At the beginning of 1917 they were more and more wound up. When they heard about the February Revolution, they went crazy. They danced all night, until our officers intervened because they were worried the enemy would take the opportunity to attack. The Tsar's abdication made them almost delirious. They couldn't stand still. You'd have thought they were going to head home straightaway."

"How did they hear this news?" Lantier asked. "You said you were cut off from the world."

"We were, but not them. And that's exactly the point. You know, we were up against the Bulgarians, and they speak pretty similar languages. They understand each other. They were all at it; the Austrians, the Turks and the

Bulgarians were getting news from Russia on a daily basis because their headquarters thought Russia's difficulties were good for their troops' morale. They promised them that once the Tsar had gone it wouldn't be long before the Russians stopped fighting the war."

"So there was contact between the Russians and the Bulgarians, when they were pitted against each other in their trenches?"

"That's what I gathered and that's what set the whole thing off . . . "

CHAPTER VII

The river was low and where the current caught on stones it produced trails of foam that whitened almost the entire surface. Willow branches that in the springtime trailed down into the water now hung in the air, still holding clods of dirty waterweeds.

The young man was crouching in the middle of the river. He'd hopped from stone to stone and now stood motionless over the flowing water, barefoot on the moss-covered rocks. His eye was steady as a hawk's, trained on the pool of water beneath him. In this small natural basin a trout snaked between the dancing bright patches the sun created on the sandy riverbed. The man slowly raised a stick sharpened to a point at one end. He waited a long while and then, in one swift action, thrust the thin lance down, skewering the fish. He drew the stick out of the water. His prey writhed around the shaft that pierced through its body. The fisherman stood up but suddenly froze like a dog pointing. He'd spotted the dark silhouette watching him on the bank.

"Don't try to make a run for it, Louis! I'll always know where to find you. Come over here."

Gabarre barely raised his voice. The river was flowing so weakly that it made little noise and the police officer's words resonated clearly in the quiet of the forest, particularly to ears practiced at picking up the least sound.

Stepping fluently from stone to stone, Louis made his way to the bank. When he reached the police sergeant he lowered his head and put his hands behind his back, trying clumsily to hide his catch. He was about twenty years old, with black eyebrows that almost met and curly hair set low on his forehead. He stood with his back stooped and a frightened look on his face whenever he met another human being. In the woods, though, his eye had all the acuity of an animal's. He lived on what he hunted and fished. His mother had died when he was ten years old, and no one really knew who his father was. He'd been sent to an orphanage and ran away twice, both times heading back to the house where he'd been born on the edge of the woods. In the end they left him there. Gabarre kept an eye on him. He knew the boy was pretty harmless but he also knew about his temptations and about his weak spot.

"Still just as agile, from what I see. Let's have a look."

The trout had stopped moving, resigned to its fate or already dead. It was a handsome fish with shimmering scales. The point of the stick had struck it exactly through the middle.

"Tell me, Louis, you're being a good boy at the moment. But you still go to see her."

The boy shook his head.

"No, no! I swear it."

"Don't swear, that's unwise. Especially as I know you do. I've been watching you too, would you believe."

Louis fiddled with the stick which was still driven through the fish.

"Listen," Gabarre went on. "I also know you haven't

done anything bad. You can't fight it, but there it is. So long as you don't disturb her anymore, you can watch her through the trees, if it makes you happy."

The young man gave a sideways glance at the police officer. He couldn't see where he was going with this conversation.

"I'd like you to help me, Louis. You owe me that at least, don't you?"

Louis waited to hear what came next before responding.

"Do you know Morlac, Valentine's sweetheart?"

A flash of loathing lit Louis's eyes.

"He went off to war," he said nastily. His diction was poor and his voice muted.

"He went off but he came back. And you know that."

Louis looked away.

"You go and see her every day, am I right?"

The young man said nothing.

"Don't go telling me lies. I know your habits. You take yourself off to the woods above her vegetable patch in the mornings, so you can watch her bend over her crops. And in the evenings you go around the back of the house to watch her when she goes to milk the goat. Don't deny it. So long as you behave yourself, I don't have any complaints."

"I only touched her once . . . "

"And you frightened her enough with that. For her to want to call me, given how little she likes uniforms, she must have had quite a scare."

"It's over now."

"I believe you, Louis. And that's not why I'm here."

"Well?"

"Well, like I said, you can help me. I want you to tell me what you know."

Louis scratched his chest with a great square paw covered in black hairs.

"Have you seen Morlac around here since he came home from the war?"

Louis was not enjoying this conversation. He obviously wanted to react the way he did best when he wasn't happy about something: by fleeing. But Gabarre was boring into him with his hard little peasant's eyes, and Louis was afraid of him.

"I think so."

"No stories, please. Did he come here, yes or no?"

"Yes."

"Several times?"

"Yes."

"How many?"

"Every day."

The police officer paused, as if he were stowing this information in a locked cupboard.

"Do you know he's in prison?"

Louis's eyes widened. A malicious smile stole over his face but he smothered it immediately.

"No. What's he done?"

"Something stupid, on Bastille Day."

"So that's why he hasn't been recently."

"When was the last time you saw him?"

"I don't know about dates. Three weeks ago, I'd say . . . "

"That makes sense. He came until the day before the parade. And what did he do when he came here? Did he talk to her?"

"Oh, no!" the young man cried out.

Gabarre sensed this was a limit that, luckily, Morlac hadn't overstepped. If he had done, the situation might have taken a different turn and, knowing Louis's suppressed violence, it could well have been dramatic.

"So, tell me. What did he do? Did he hide like you and watch her?"

"I'm better at hiding than him. He didn't see me."

"What about her, do you think she saw him?"

"I'd be surprised. It wasn't her he was following."

"Who then?"

"The kid."

Gabarre took a step back and sat down on the trunk of a felled tree that lay along the bank. The heat was encroaching toward the river, despite the cool air coming off the water. He mopped his brow with a large checkered handkerchief folded into eighths.

"Are you sure about this? It was the kid he was watching?"

"Why would I lie?"

"Did he try to talk to him?"

"No."

"He didn't talk to him or he didn't try?"

"He didn't try."

The police officer heaved a sigh. Conversations with Louis were always littered with traps like that. The boy's mind didn't grasp nuances. He took words at face value. You couldn't hold it against him. But it was trying.

"Do you mean he actually did? He talked to the kid, is that right?"

"Yes."

"How did it happen?"

"It was one morning. She was in the house."

Louis always said "she," as if her name, Valentine, was too violent, too painful.

"The kid had gone off to play near the château."

This was the name the locals used to give to the ruins of a fortified house, which, it was claimed, had been the home of Agnès Sorel, mistress to the fifteenth-century king Charles VII. The name was used less and less because the ruins in question were now just a pile of loose stones and brambles. But Louis stuck to the old ways.

"Did you follow them?"

"Of course. The kid *is* kind of her, you know."

Gabarre realized the poor simpleton cherished the foolish notion that, by protecting Valentine's son, he could earn her gratitude and perhaps her love.

"What did they say to each other?"

"I was too far away. I couldn't hear. This guy of yours, Morlac, he came out of hiding and talked for a long time. The kid listened to him but when Morlac tried to take his hand the little critter did what I'd have done, Lord knows. He scrammed."

"Did Morlac try again after that?"

"Once. But when the kid saw him he didn't let him get near. He ran off."

"Do you think he told his mother about it?"

"I'd be surprised."

"What makes you think that?"

"If he'd said something then she wouldn't have let him carry on going out on his own. Yes, that's why I think he didn't tell her anything: so he could carry on running about wherever he liked. Well, that's what I'd have done in his situation."

The police officer nodded and then stood up, came

over to Louis and pinched his ear. It was what Napoleon used to do to his soldiers, and Gabarre knew this. But, after all, what harm was there in copying the emperor's finer characteristics? Louis was used to this liberty, and saw it for what it was: an encouraging gesture, a sign of praise.

"You'd better expect to see me back soon!" trilled the police sergeant.

But the phrase was all part of the ritual, and Louis knew that months could go by without him hearing a word from Gabarre. He affected a respectful and slightly frightened expression to make it look as if he'd learned his lesson. Then, not waiting to hear more, he slunk off with his trout.

* * *

The sun had gone so Morlac and the major were now walking around the yard, with their hands in their front pockets, making the fabric bulge out of shape.

"After the February Revolution the Russians started bickering," the prisoner said.

"The Tsarists with the revolutionaries, I imagine?"

"There weren't many Tsarists. Maybe among the officers, but they kept quiet at any rate. No, the squabble was between the supporters of the provisional government and the Soviets who wanted to carry on with the revolution. Afoninov was all for the Soviets."

"And you?"

"Me?"

Morlac looked flustered. He knew he'd have to talk about himself. He took responsibility for his role in this business. But it was how it started that he seemed to find difficult. How could he explain the way he'd ended up in the whole thing?

"You know, in the early days, I never thought one day I'd have to use the books I'd read."

"The books you'd read at Valentine's house?"

Morlac didn't want to answer and, on this occasion, Lantier felt it was tactless of him to have been so unnecessarily blunt.

"When I was on leave I read a lot. The war had changed me. I couldn't have imagined all that sort of thing existed: shelling, hordes of people in uniform, fighting where, in a matter of minutes, thousands of men lay dead in the sunlight. I was just a little peasant, you see? I didn't know anything. Even though I started reading before the war, they were meaningless books. When I came back on leave it was different: I needed to find answers. I wanted to see what other people had managed to make of war and society and the army, power, money, all the things I was just discovering."

"How long were you here on leave?"

"Two weeks. Nothing like enough. But the books I didn't get around to reading I took with me."

"You can't get many into a kit bag."

"I took three."

"What were they?"

Morlac stood tall as he gave the titles, as if announcing the Gospel.

"Proudhon's *Philosophy of Poverty*, Marx's *The Eighteenth Brumaire*, and Kropotkin's *Anarchist Morality*."

"Didn't you have problems with material like that in your bag?"

"The staff actually only started worrying after the Russian Revolution. And I'd taken my precautions. I'd changed the covers. From the outside they looked like romantic novels."

Lantier thought about Valentine's father, well versed in clandestine tricks. His daughter had been taught to hide things from a very young age. She must have rather liked introducing Morlac to this territory, sharing these dangerous secrets with him.

"And what did you find in these books?"

"When they explained the world, I understood what they were saying. But I thought their ideas on revolution were just pipe dreams or, in a pinch, a promise for the afterlife, like paradise. With the events in Russia, I realized it was all possible."

Morlac had come to a halt and was looking Lantier squarely in the face. He was transformed. There was no cheerfulness in him, no, still none of that, only a sort of radiance coming from within him. His eyes were more ardent and he breathed more deeply, his skin was colored by a sudden rush of blood. This was no longer a peasant with blinkered thoughts about his land, but a man full of eagerness for expansion and the future. If it weren't for what he was saying, he could have been mistaken for a lunatic.

"Just think. We were in the pit of hell, in a cesspool. The world had descended into barbarity. But at the same time there was a place where the will of the people had allowed a nation to rid itself of a tyrant. We had to finish what was started. We had to carry on with the revolution, not just in Russia but everywhere. And to do that, the first thing we had to do was end this war. If we revolted, the generals would be left to sort it out on their own . . . We could bring them down using the same methods that got the better of Nicolas II."

"Did you take part in the mutinies?"

Lantier was surprised he'd seen no mention of this in the prisoner's military file. Quite the opposite, it was in 1917 that Morlac had been decorated for an act of heroism.

"No," Morlac confirmed.

"Were there any in your unit?"

"Stupid gestures. Several boys mutilated themselves in order to be evacuated. Selfish little creeps who wanted to save their own skins. They thought they were clever but they were usually found out, they were judged and sometimes they were shot. What was the difference?"

Lantier had had experience of an incident like this in his unit during the war: A young baker's assistant had managed to lose two fingers by brandishing his arm over the top of his trench while on night guard duty. The lines had been very close together. Some poor fellow on the other side must have realized what he wanted and fired. It was a sordid affair but, as platoon commander, Lantier had had no choice but to send the kid off to a court-martial. He didn't know what had happened to him.

"With the Russians we had other ideas. We saw things on a bigger scale."

The disturbing side of Morlac's character was now out in the daylight. So far Lantier hadn't managed to grasp the source of the wariness mingled with fascination that the prisoner inspired in him. And now, all of a sudden, he understood: It was this combination of reserve and megalomania, his feigned modesty and his profound conviction that he was cleverer than everyone else. Morlac was a dwarf consumed with giant-sized ambitions. It was hard to know whether to pity him for keeping such huge ideals shut away inside him, or laugh at his pretention in embracing such intentions.

"Along with Afoninov and his friends, we developed a very ambitious plan which involved the Bulgarians. Our reasoning was straightforward: For a movement of resistance to the war to be efficient, it had to develop on both sides of the front. Otherwise, it would turn into defeat for one side or the other, and the men who refused to fight would be called traitors. What we wanted was first fraternization and then disobedience."

"They happened in France, too, these truces between soldiers at the front. I've heard about an incident like that one Christmas."

"Yes, there was fraternizing," Morlac agreed earnestly. "But, without political foundations, it couldn't go far. That's why we wanted to put pressure on men who had the same revolutionary ideas as us."

"You had officers, men in command. Did they let you get on with it? Did they have the same ideas as you?"

The prisoner gave a small contemptuous smile.

"We weren't going to take pointless risks and try to rally class enemies to our cause. We only used clandestine methods. Officially, I was going over to the Russians to drink and listen to their music. I had my dog, which was convenient: I told my sergeant that Wilhelm was constantly parked over there because he'd found a girlfriend, which was true. And he gave me permission to go and fetch him."

"Did the Russians have dogs, too?"

"I don't know where she came from; they may have found her there. Either way, they had a mascot with them, a bitch they called Sabaka. Wilhelm was much bigger than her but he somehow managed to get her in pup. I left before she whelped and I don't know what they ended up looking like."

Dujeux came into the courtyard and announced that the prisoner's lunch had arrived. They went back to the cell. Realizing the interrogation was to go on a long time, the jailer had set up a small table with two plates and two glasses. The major sat down opposite Morlac and they continued with their discussion while they ate the warm stew that Dujeux had poured from the tin pot delivered to him.

"So this plan, then?"

"It was simple but quite difficult to realize. There was a sector, near Fort Rupel, where the Bulgarian lines and our own were very close. It wasn't like that everywhere. In that mountainous territory we mostly had isolated outposts fairly far apart. With their runners, the Russians knew the Bulgarian units were relieved every ten days. One particular unit had a lot of soldiers committed to the cause. The idea was to wait till they came to the front. Once they were in their trenches there'd be a signal, the Bulgarian troops would kill their officers and we'd come out and fraternize. Supporters all along the front would spread the news and organize the uprising. We'd send proclamations to Salonika and Sofia. Civilian workers would revolt. It would be the end of the war and the beginning of the revolution."

"Eat," said Lantier. "It'll get cold."

Morlac looked at his plate and seemed to take a

moment to readjust. He gulped down his stew, keen to get such everyday matters out of the way.

"And what actually happened in the end?"

The prisoner's face darkened. He set down his spoon slowly and tore off some bread to clean his plate.

"It went as planned, to start with."

There was a pause. Morlac was his gloomy self again and his stubborn expression was back.

"It took nearly three weeks of preparations. I had to find an excuse to go over to the Russian lines when the time for action came. There was some hitch in the rotation of Bulgarian troops. In the end everything fell into place on September 12."

"I thought that was the day you earned your mention?"

Morlac shrugged without replying. He sat back and ran a fingernail between two side teeth.

"It was beautiful night. It had been a hot day. Everyone felt confident, rested. But there was a lot of tension. The tricky bit was going out into no-man's-land. Unfortunately, there was no moon that night, and you couldn't see much. We'd got the wire cutters ready to cut the barbed wire. Once contact had been made we could light lamps and organize ourselves. The most dangerous bit was the beginning."

"How many of you were in on it?"

"On the Russian side almost the whole unit. Afoninov had assured me that on the Bulgarian side there were at least two hundred men who'd go for it. On top of that, the timing was good because the officers from that sector had been summoned to headquarters."

Dujeux came in to clear the plates. He put an apple in front of each of them and left.

"We'd planned the action for four o'clock. That meant we could get things organized before sunrise but we wouldn't be in the dark for too long once both camps were united."

"What was the signal?"

"*The Internationale*. They would sing it on the Bulgarian side and we'd join in in chorus. Our positions were so close we could hear everything, especially at night. At four o'clock we heard the hymn wafting over from their lines. You can't imagine the effect it had on us."

The major thought Morlac's eyes looked watery. In any event, he took out a handkerchief and hid his emotion by blowing into it.

"Then everything happened very quickly. At the time we didn't understand what was going on. It was only afterwards that we put it all together."

He blew his nose again, noisily this time. And resumed his irritable expression.

"I'll spare you the details. It all started with Wilhelm. He was with me, as usual. He has good eyesight and a hunting dog's instinct. When he realized there was movement in the enemy lines, he climbed onto the parapet and out of the trench. One of the Bulgarians came forward, as planned. But the dog wasn't in on the plan . . . " Morlac paused to snigger. "He jumped at the man's throat. He'd done it before when we had that skirmish with bayonets, and he'd been praised, hadn't he? To him an enemy was an enemy. He's a good loyal dog."

Morlac's face was contorting into a hideous grimace.

"Yes, loyal," he said again.

Lantier was beginning to understand.

"The Bulgarian screamed. And there in the darkness

everyone lost their heads. The most committed to the cause could shout as much as they liked that it was meaningless, the others didn't believe them. They thought we'd set a trap for them. Some started shooting. There was some return fire from our lines. People threw up flares. The artillery on our side reacted quickly and sprayed the Bulgarian trenches. I don't need to draw you a diagram . . . "

"How did you extricate yourselves?"

"Afoninov and I were horrified. At first we held the boys back. But then things took a different turn. It was war again. Every man for himself. Someone gave the signal to attack. The Russians went over the top with me. The Bulgarians had prepared the mutiny carefully: They'd eliminated all the NCOs in the sector. Their lines were a complete shambles and we broke through them without any resistance. It was terrible. We were killing comrades who were just about to join us. A few minutes earlier we'd been prepared to fraternize but now we were in attack mode, we killed everyone we came across."

"And eventually you were injured?"

"After an hour, or thereabouts. We'd broken through three lines of defense and our artillery hadn't anticipated we'd advance that far. They started using heavy shells and I took some shrapnel in the back of my head. It wasn't deep but it knocked me out. I woke up three days later in Salonika, in the hospital."

CHAPTER VIII

T hat's how I became a hero."
To punctuate this conclusion, Morlac took a savage
bite of his apple.

"Because of the dog, when it comes down to it," suggested the major.

The prisoner nodded as he chewed.

"Is that why you hate Wilhelm?"

"I don't hate him anymore," he said, spitting out a pip.
"Okay, when I came round in the hospital, that was another
story: When I realized what had happened I felt like killing
him. As soon as I could get up I saw him down below, in
the courtyard, waiting for me. And for nights on end, till
the end of my convalescence, I tried to picture how I could
get rid of him."

Morlac threw the core onto the table.

"But I couldn't do it. First of all, I was stuck in bed.
But mostly because I was a hero, you see? Officers had
come to bring me my mention signed by Sarrail himself.
When General Guillaumat took over from him, he visited the hospital and came into my ward with his staff to
congratulate me. Everyone kept talking about my dog.
They knew he'd been at the front with me. The nurses
fed him in the yard and told me how he was doing. No
one would have understood if I'd gotten rid of him with

a pistol. But that was what I thought about day and night."

He sniggered as he talked, wearing the bitter expression that so irritated Lantier.

"I spent the whole winter cooped up, being tended to. But with the first good weather, the doctors thought they were doing me a favor saying I could go out for walks. And those idiotic nurses brought Wilhelm to me to keep me company! They'd even clubbed together to buy him a smart collar. The only consolation I had for having to tolerate him was seeing his face on the end of a leash!"

"But he's a dog, you can't hold it against him . . . "

"That's what I ended up thinking. It took me nearly six months. It was high summer, I remember it like it was yesterday. We were sitting in the shade of an umbrella pine, him and me. I was looking at his neck, the skin was peeling because he'd been injured too in this whole thing, and it was taking a while to scar. And all of a sudden I felt kind of dizzy. It felt like everything was spinning around me. But it was all going on inside my head: Everything was suddenly falling into place. A massive shake-up in my mind."

He stood up and walked to the far end of the cell, then spun round fiercely.

"*He* was the hero. That's what I thought, you see. Not just because he followed me to the front and was wounded. No, it was deeper than that, more radical. He had all the good qualities expected of soldiers. He was loyal to the death, brave, merciless toward his enemies. To him, the world's made up of goodies and baddies. There was another way of putting this: He had no humanity. Of course, he was a dog . . . But *we* weren't dogs and they were expecting the same from us. The distinctions, medals, mentions, promotions, all that was designed to reward animal behavior."

He was now standing facing Lantier but looking beyond him, above him, which, in the confines of this cell, meant staring at the wall.

"On the other hand, the only demonstration of humanity—the one that involved getting enemies to fraternize, to lay down their weapons and force governments to agree to peace—that act was the most reprehensible of all and would have cost us our lives if we'd been found out."

He waited a moment, calmed himself and went and sat back down.

"When I realized that," he went on, "I stopped hating Wilhelm. I didn't have any reason to love him either. He'd obeyed his own nature and that wasn't human nature. That was his only excuse. But everyone who sent us off to that massacre had no excuse at all. Anyway, that's when I decided what I would do."

Lantier had sat in silence through this long explanation. He was profoundly shaken. Deep down, he understood everything Morlac said and agreed with it. And yet, had this prisoner been brought before him for desertion or mutiny, he would have condemned him to death without hesitation.

The prisoner was exhausted by his confession. He sat on the edge of the bed with his arms hanging limply by his sides, and a blank stare on his face. His judge was no more alert than he was, but felt a need to get out of this airless room, to walk about, to put his thoughts into some sort of order. He'd been investigating this case for four days now, and it was time he reached a firm conclusion. After all, he mustn't grant this character and his actions more significance than they actually had.

Lantier was known for his ability to act decisively, even in the most sensitive of cases. This time, though, he couldn't do it. The more he learned about the case, the more his opinion floundered. He wondered briefly whether Morlac was deliberately scrambling his thoughts. But that meant denying the obvious sincerity of his confession.

The major's annoyance made him react, for once, without consideration for the defendant. He took his leave curtly with the words, "Be prepared to sign the written statement of your hearing tomorrow."

Once he was back outside on the Place Michelet, which was still warm from the sun that had bathed it, Lantier rubbed his hand over his face and stared around him, like someone waking from a nightmare.

The first living thing he saw was Wilhelm, who had resumed his post under the trees. The dog didn't bark, but tracked him with his eyes until he turned at the end of the street.

* * *

Valentine didn't smoke, usually. But her initiative had unsettled her and she'd chosen this means of unwinding. Lantier had passed her his packet of shag, and she coughed as she inhaled deeply on her badly rolled cigarette.

He'd come across her as he stepped into the hotel lobby, and she'd asked to speak with him again. This time, however, it was not for a brief conversation. She wanted to tell him something confidentially and, with the brazenness of the shy, she barely disguised her hope that he would invite her to dine with him. He couldn't care less what people said and neither, apparently, could she. He'd taken her to the restaurant where he'd met the attorney-at-law. The place was completely empty this time. She was desperately trying to look detached but her eyes shone brightly. She stroked the smooth, white fabric of her table napkin like the soft pelt of an animal.

"It's not like me to confide in a man in uniform. You must have done some research. You know my background."

She'd drunk half the bottle of Bordeaux in a quarter of an hour. Lantier definitely didn't want her to think he was trying to get her drunk. But she knew what she was doing. Strange though it might seem, she was still perfectly in control of herself, perhaps more so than when she'd had nothing to drink.

"When I met him he'd hardly set foot outside his farm."

The subject was Morlac, clearly. Lantier would cheerfully have done without this. He wanted to be on his own and forget the whole business. But there it was; he wasn't done with it. He might as well see it through to the end and listen to what she had to say.

"What did I like about him? Why did I take an interest in him?"

He hadn't asked her anything. It was this sort of supposition that proved to him she was a little tipsy. She was actually talking to herself.

"He didn't look like a country type, that was it. There are people like that, who don't live in their true class. That's quite reassuring, wouldn't you say? I'd had my head filled with stuff about the class struggle. All through my childhood my father talked of nothing else. I accepted the idea. It's the truth; there's no denying it. But when he died and I ended up here, in the country, I thought that wasn't enough. There were individuals, too. The things that happen to them can make them change class, like with me, for example. And then there are those who seem to live outside all that, sort of just by being themselves."

She'd hardly touched her beef and onion stew. She probably wasn't used to eating meat, or sauces.

"When we met, Jacques could only just read. He learned to read properly to please me, I know that. It embarrassed me but at the same time I liked the thought that he'd gone to that trouble for me. It was proof of his love. He didn't know how to talk about love but he'd found this way of saying what he felt."

"What did he read?"

"Anything. Mostly novels. He didn't say what sort of thing he liked but I saw the gaps on the shelves when he left. I've always known where my books are. You wouldn't think so to look at them. They don't look organized. But I know."

In this hot weather it was more obvious how thin she was. She wore a clumsily knitted little cardigan over her dress but, what with the heat of the wine, she'd taken it off and Lantier could see her neck with its clearly defined muscles, and the hollows around her collarbones where the straps of her bodice slid over them.

"I had *The New Heloise*, because it was Rousseau and my father saw him as the great thinker of the Enlightenment. But I knew that Jacques was keeping it such a long time for another reason. He was romantic, without realizing it. And I liked that."

"Did you not talk to him about politics?"

"Never, at that point. When war was declared we talked about the situation one time. He was incredibly naïve. To be honest, he didn't know anything. In that way, he was definitely a country boy. He just accepted that one day they'd come and get him to fight, even though he didn't like it. When he left I tried to talk to him. But I realized it was pointless. I found myself doing things I would never have imagined. I knitted him a scarf. I wanted him to go with something of me. I was really happy when my dog left with him."

"Is Wilhelm your dog?"

"That wasn't his name then. He was my great-aunt's dog, or rather the son of her old Briard bitch. We'd drowned the others but my aunt kept that one for me. I called him Kirou."

She was laughing now but, mindful of her appearance, she never showed her teeth for long because she had one missing on the side and she knew it didn't look pretty.

"That dog really liked men. Every time the postman came he followed him, and it was often several days before he came home. When Jacques started coming over Kirou would make a fuss of him."

"Did you tell him to take the dog to war with him?"

"As if! He went of his own accord. And I was glad of it."

"Did he send you news?"

"While he was in France I received letters every week. And one day he came back."

The bottle was empty. Lantier couldn't make up his mind to buy another. She was breaking up her piece of bread and nibbling on bits of crust.

"It was late December. The weather was very cold. That damp cold we get here. We stayed inside in the warm all day and all night. I burned all the wood I'd put aside for the winter. It didn't bother me. I wanted him to be comfortable."

"Had he changed?"

"Completely. He was like a tree with no leaves, all hard and dried out. He'd stopped smiling. And talked a lot."

"About what?"

"About the fighting, even though he wasn't at the front at that point. About all the men he'd met in the army. About the unbelievable weapons that had been invented to kill people. He didn't understand any of it. The war was a mystery to him. He'd never imagined it could exist. He wanted to know. Politics, economics, peoples, nations, he'd started thinking about everything."

She had picked up her glass and was looking forlornly at the dregs of wine left in it. Lantier ordered another bottle.

"I didn't want to talk to him about abstract things like that. It might be difficult to understand. But, you see, I was in love and that was all I wanted to think about. I knew he wouldn't be here long. I wanted to be happy. I wanted to kiss him and touch him and hold him close to me. So I settled for recommending books to him. He started reading political material he hadn't been interested in till then. And while he read I watched him, I smothered him with kisses, I basked in his warmth."

"How long did he stay?"

"Two weeks. Obviously I was pregnant. I knew it

would happen. I wanted it to. I could almost tell you when our child was conceived. But I didn't say anything to him."

The waitress had come back with the new bottle. She filled the glasses with a surly expression and spilled some wine on the tablecloth without apologizing.

"He took three books with him when he left."

"Proudhon, Marx, and Kropotkin."

"He told you."

For the first time since their conversation started she looked intently at Lantier and he felt she was only now acknowledging he was there.

"After that," he said, "he went to join the Oriental Expeditionary Force."

She suddenly looked very weary. Her whole face crumpled as if an intense pain had come back to grip her insides.

"That's what he wrote and told me. I felt helpless. You see, so long as he was in France I felt he was still near. But with the war in Greece it was completely different. I had this feeling he'd never come back. I sent him a letter to tell him I was expecting a child. I felt he had to know before he left. Maybe deep down I was hoping he'd find some way to stay close to me."

"How did he take the news?"

"He wrote to say it was a good thing, and told me to call the baby Marie if it was a girl and Jules if it was a boy, in case it was born before he came back."

She gave a nervous laugh. "Like I said, he doesn't know how to express his feelings."

Lantier thought he saw a tear glistening in the corner of her eye but she flicked her head to toss her hair back, and everything disappeared.

"So then I realized there was only one hope: for the war to end as soon as possible. I'd distanced myself from my father's former friends. I didn't want to hear any more about them. Politics had done us enough harm. But I suddenly changed my mind. The only people fighting against the war—the ones who'd immediately pronounced it a disgrace, who'd dissected what had caused it and wanted to deal with the problem at the very root—were these utopians and socialist agitators, and I'd been wrong to look down on them. I wrote to one of them, a man called Gendrot, who was my godfather. He'd tried to see me after my father died but I'd never answered his letters. Luckily he was still at the same address and my letter reached him."

Three men had come into the bar, which was cut off from the restaurant by a frosted glass partition that stopped short of the ceiling. They could be heard chatting loudly with the landlord.

"This Gendrot worked closely with Jaurès. After Jaurès's assassination, Gendrot stayed faithful to his pacifist ideas. He had problems with the army."

Lantier was glad to see that she no longer seemed to identify him with the army. She was confiding in him and making allowances.

"He carried on running a very active group against the war. They had official activities, with a newspaper that was pretty much censored. But he also took care of supporting pacifist militants, particularly foreigners who needed to hide."

"Weren't you afraid you might have trouble yourself by contacting him?"

"What sort of trouble? I've always been watched, you

know, because of my father. But the police know I don't do any harm. I didn't say much in my message, anyway, except that I wanted to see him again because he was still my godfather, after all."

"Did he reply?"

"He sent someone. A miner from Creusot who traveled sixty miles on foot to come and talk to me. He stayed two days. He saw where I lived and realized how I could help them."

"Didn't they want you to move into town?"

"Absolutely not. They needed hideouts deep in the country for boys on the run or who needed to be forgotten."

"Did you write and tell Morlac this?"

They'd ordered coffee, she'd let two sugar lumps dissolve slowly in hers and was now stirring it.

"Unfortunately not. I didn't want him to worry. I was doing it for me, you see, so that I felt useful, to contribute, just a bit, to cutting short the war."

"Had he already left for Greece?"

"I didn't know. The mail was getting very irregular. Jacques was trundled from one camp to another, farther and farther south. In the end they took them to Toulon. But the sailing kept being postponed, because of the submarine war."

She pulled a face. The drunken cries from the bar were growing louder and smothered her words from time to time because she was speaking quietly.

"Anyway, Gendrot didn't waste any time. He had packets of clandestine tracts delivered to me, and I had to hide them until they were distributed. He sent a couple of Belgians who'd escaped from an internment camp. For those six months there were people in the house practically the whole time."

"And Morlac still didn't know?"

She looked down. It was clearly painful for her reliving this time. She was wringing her fingers agitatedly.

"I didn't tell him anything. Now that I was actually doing something I couldn't possibly give away any details in my letters. There was military censorship . . . But it's true, I should have warned him all the same. It would have stopped him finding out for himself."

"Finding out? How could he possibly know when he was so far away?"

"He came back."

"You mean he had a second period of leave?"

"In July, shortly before they sailed, he managed to get three days' leave. He didn't say where he was going; they'd never have allowed it. He performed miracles, jumping onto freight trains, stealing a horse, walking the last few miles till his shoes fell apart. I only found all that out later . . . "

She was laughing in admiration, regret, despair.

"He arrived at dawn. He hid behind the little wall around the vegetable plot. Do you know where I mean? He wanted to surprise me."

She sniffed and straightened in her chair, to gather her composure.

"At the time Gendrot had sent me a laborer from Alsace who was being hunted down for sabotage. He was a great tall gentle boy. He didn't say much but helped me a lot. With the pregnancy there were some jobs in the garden I couldn't do. This Albert knew how to work a vegetable patch. I didn't even have to tell him what needed doing."

"You only have one room. Where did he sleep?"

She looked up, defiantly.

"With me. We didn't do anything. I wasn't far off my time anyway. But, you see, I don't know if a man can understand this, I needed someone there. I huddled up against him. I was no longer alone. And my child was no longer alone either. It feels strange saying it."

"And was he happy with that?"

"I think so. He was very gentle. He covered me with kisses. Sometimes I could feel he wanted me, but he never forced me. He told me a bit of tenderness was enough for him. It pained him terribly being away from his family. A family of women, as it happens, his mother and four sisters."

"Did Morlac find you together?"

"He saw Albert come out of the house, because he always got up before me to go and wash by the well."

"Did the boy know you had a lover away at war?"

"He guessed, given my condition. But the rule, with comrades, is to say as little as possible about yourself, in case anyone's interrogated."

"Did the two of them talk?"

"When Albert spotted a soldier in the vegetable plot he wanted to know what he was doing there. Morlac asked whether I was at home. Albert said I was still asleep."

She'd wound her table napkin around her fingers and was pulling it tighter and tighter. The blood couldn't get through. It must have been very painful.

"Albert asked whether there was any message. Jacques stood up to his full height, looked over at the closed door for a moment and said 'no.' Then he left."

"And you didn't see him?"

"I was very tired that day. The baby kicked a lot. I hadn't slept well. I got up an hour later. Albert had gone to cut some grass for the rabbits. He told me about Morlac's visit over lunch. It was too late to catch up with him."

Lantier looked at her. Despite her thinness, the fact she took so little care of herself and the marks left on her face by her ordeals, there was a spark about her that made her beautiful, like a fire that won't go out, a light that shines all the brighter for being in total darkness.

"Did you write to him?"

"Of course. But again, because of censorship, I couldn't explain the situation exactly as it was. And anyway, I wasn't even sure he was receiving my letters."

"Didn't he send you any?"

"Never again."

"Did you tell him when your son was born?"

"When Jules was born I wrote to him. And a bit later I even managed to have a photo taken in town. I don't know whether it reached him."

This time, despite her efforts, she couldn't hold back her tears. They fell silently and rolled like raindrops over dry wood. She let three or four fall before reacting. She rubbed her napkin over her cheeks, then looked Lantier squarely in the face as she said, "I can assure you, sir, that I've never stopped thinking about him. I've only ever loved him. I love only him. I dream about him. Sometimes, on winter nights, I'd go out in the cold, without putting any clothes on, without even feeling the frost, and I'd scream his name, as if he might turn up there, among the vegetables, and come back to me. I closed my eyes and I could feel his breath, I could smell him . . . You think I'm crazy."

Lantier looked down. The screams of a woman in love always left men feeling that, in this domain, they were much the weaker sex.

"Did you not know he was back when he came home after the war?"

"Not until he created this scandal and was arrested."

The drunks in the other room were tumbling outside. The waitress hovered in the half-open doorway, to see whether she should bring in the check.

"I'm depending on you," said Valentine, staring the major in the eye pointedly.

CHAPTER IX

Before tackling the final stage of his inquiry, Lantier felt a need to take a long walk through the countryside.

He rose at dawn and set off north, toward the beginnings of the large forest that stretched all the way to Bourges.

The trees were mostly oaks. The first of them had been planted as far back as the reign of Louis XIV. As a walker heads deeper along the forest paths he'll come across areas where the trees are unexpectedly aligned. Here the random arrangement of trunks briefly gives way to rectilinear pockets that seem to reach all the way to the horizon. This sudden mark of human will amid the chaos of nature is not unlike the birth of an idea in the magma of ill-defined thought. All at once, in both cases, a perspective emerges, a corridor of light that brings order to solid things as it does to ideas, and allows for a more far-reaching view. In both instances, these moments of illumination are short-lived. As soon as the walker sets off again, as soon as the mind starts churning again, the vision vanishes, unless it has been committed to memory or written down.

All the same, walking through a forest like this is a powerful stimulant for thought. Lantier needed it. As well as the investigation keeping him here, he was thinking about the life that lay in store for him, the new phase he would step into when he left military life. He thought about this war that was drawing to an end for a second time, with these last few trials. Cemeteries as rectilinear as those pockets in the trees had been built on the battlefields to shelter the remains of dead soldiers. But those particular seeds would never grow.

He found a pond deep in the forest and walked around it. He came across hunting men patrolling through the woods in preparation for the coming season. They were preceded by their dogs, who came and sniffed at Lantier. It occurred to him that a dog was the only company that didn't disturb solitude. He thought about Wilhelm and felt that, through his hardships, Morlac had certainly been lucky to have this animal by his side the whole time. And he resented him for showing so little gratitude.

Next he went down onto a plain sown with barley, and walked along the edge of the fields, which undulated with a swell of blond tufts. He ended up on a dusty track that headed back toward town. He'd barely walked two hundred yards along it before he spotted someone coming toward him on a bicycle. It was Gabarre.

"I was looking for you. They said you were around here."

The solitude was at an end. The police officer walked up to Lantier, pushing his bicycle. He told him what he had learned.

The fellow was as faithful as Wilhelm, Lantier thought to himself. But even so, going for a walk with a policeman doesn't have quite the same effect . . .

* * *

Dujeux was cursing the major, who'd asked him to stand guard outside. What sort of idea was that to interrogate the prisoner out of his cell and sit him down in the office! All right, so it was the last day. The man had to sign a written statement and hear the military investigating officer's decision. But all the same, what an idea . . . He'd walked roughshod over the regulations and if things went awry, Dujeux would be sure to make it clear it was nothing to do with him.

Lantier was sitting behind the desk and the defendant sat facing him in a stick-back chair with one armrest missing.

"I've done a lot of thinking, Morlac. Permit me to say that the idea you've formed of humanity is somewhat incomplete."

"What do you mean?"

"This business of fraternizing, the mutiny you were hoping to organize, the end of the war . . . "

"Yes?"

"That's what you see as humanity, isn't it? Fraternity to counter hatred and all that."

"It is."

"Well, it falls a bit short, I think. Humanity also means having an ideal and fighting for it. You were in favor of peace because you didn't believe in this war. You're against the concept of a nation and against bourgeois governments. Am I right?"

Morlac was slightly wrong-footed because he hadn't expected the conversation to start like this, and he was on his guard.

"But it strikes me," the major continued, "that if it were a question of fighting for ideals in which you did believe, you'd agree to it. When the Russian revolutionaries took power in October, didn't you cheer them on?"

"Yes."

"And when the Tsar's family were killed, did you appeal for fraternization?"

"It was the price that had to be paid to quash a reaction."

"Ah, I see! The price that had to be paid . . . "

Lantier stood up and turned toward the window, with his hands behind his back.

"Let's drop the subject. We could spend a long time talking about it, I'm sure of that," he said, then spun round around and stared at the prisoner as he added, "I just wanted things to be clear. We don't have the same values, we don't believe in the same ideas. But we're both fighting men."

"If you like. So?"

"So, in my opinion, what you did, the act for which I must judge you, was a mistake from the point of view of your particular fight."

Morlac's astonishment was clear to see.

"A mistake and a weakness, if I may say. There's nothing coherent about your action in relation to the fight you're fighting and which, should I need to remind you, is not the same as mine."

"I don't understand what you're saying."

"You don't understand. Well, let's look back at the facts."

Lantier sat down and opened the file on the desk.

"'On July 14, 1919,'" he read, "'at 08:30 hours, while the

procession was gathering on Danton Avenue, one Jacques Morlac approached the VIP stand where representatives of constitutional bodies had already taken their seats to either side of Mr. Émile Legagneur, the regional prefect. The above named Morlac is a veteran from a farming family and is held in very high regard locally. In consideration of his injuries and the Légion d'honneur he was awarded in combat, the police officer on duty next to the stand saw no need to ask him to step aside.'"

Morlac shrugged, staring blankly into space.

"'The above named Morlac walked right up to the prefect and stopped less than three paces from the VIP stand. The guests of honor then fell completely silent. The above named Morlac addressed the authorities in a loud voice and stated his identity.'"

Lantier looked up to check the prisoner was listening.

"'Then, without using notes, he gave the following speech, which he had clearly premeditated and learned by heart: *For his exemplary conduct on the Eastern Front, showing no hesitation in attacking a Bulgarian soldier although the latter was driven only by pacifist intentions, the soldier Wilhelm here present before you has earned his country's highest recognition.*'"

Morlac let slip a sad smile.

"'The above named Morlac then took the medal and added: *Soldier Wilhelm, in the name of the President of France, I do hereby grant you access to the order of ignominy which rewards blind violence, submission to leaders and the basest of instincts, and I appoint you as a Knight of the Légion d'honneur.* He hung the decoration around the dog's neck, performed a military salute and did an about-turn so that he was in line with the parade. The first of the troops were drawing level with the stand at this point. The above named Morlac marched at the head of the procession, just behind his absurdly decorated dog.'"

As if he'd heard his name, Wilhelm yapped twice feebly from the far end of the square.

"'The crowd that had gathered on the esplanade suddenly became aware of this provocative act and exploded with laughter and jeering. The words "Down with war" were heard. There were bursts of applause. The events happened very quickly and the policeman on duty did not hear the above named Morlac's speech; it was therefore not possible to bring a timely end to the public disgrace he had decided to inflict on the authorities. Squadron Sergeant-Major Gabarre was posted at some distance from the stand and witnessed the above mentioned Morlac and the dog with its red sash processing grotesquely at the head of the troops, and Gabarre proceeded to arrest him. This action, although legitimate, triggered demonstrations of hostility within the crowd. Stones were thrown at the Squadron Sergeant-Major and he sustained a light injury to the temple. The prefect ordered for the crowd to be dispersed, and had to ask the troops to intervene in the ceremonial uniforms they were wearing for the parade. The ceremony came to an end before this year's solemn homage owed to the nation had been pronounced.'"

Lantier sat up and pushed aside the file.

"Do you want me to sign it?" Morlac asked with the same lax smile.

"Do you know what an action like that could cost you?"

"What does it matter. Have me shot, if you want."

"We're no longer at war and the law won't be so expeditious. But deportation is the most likely sanction."

"Well then, send me to the penal colony. I'm ready for it."

"You're ready for it and you seem to want it, I've seen that. I've known that from the start. You refuse every solution I've suggested to mitigate your actions and secure clemency. Let's talk about that, then, shall we? Why do you want to be condemned? Do you really think that will serve your cause?"

"Anything that fills the people with disgust for war is good for the cause I defend, like you say. If so-called heroes refused the abject honors handed out by the men who organized the butchery, we'd stop celebrating what's claimed to be a victory. The only victory worth having is the one we need to win against the war and against the capitalists who wanted it."

The major stood up, came around to the front of his desk and went to sit in a chair facing Morlac. Their legs were almost touching.

"Just how convinced are you by what you say?"

Confronted with the officer's smile, Morlac was unsettled.

"I believe it, that's the long and the short of it."

"Well, *I* say that you don't. You've put together your argument and you're standing by it. But you don't believe in it."

"Why?"

"Because you're not sufficiently naïve to think your little flash in the pan will change the world."

"It's a start."

"No, it's an end. For you, at least. You're going to disappear off to some distant colony to break stones, and you'll never come back."

"What difference does it make to you?"

"To me, none. But we're talking about you. Your 'cause' will lose one of its defenders. You'll have fired your only cartridge without touching anyone, and the cause in question won't have moved forward an inch."

"If you condemn me, the people will revolt."

"Do you think so? You made people laugh, granted. But of all those who applauded you, how many would take up arms to defend you? If you hadn't done anything, the same people would have cheered the parade. The people you put so much confidence in are tired of fighting, even against the war. Soon they'll be walking past the monuments to the dead with complete indifference."

"The revolution will come."

"Let's say you're right and that it's a necessary thing. How do you think the establishment is toppled? By decorating a dog in front of a prefect?"

There was no contempt in Lantier's voice. Which made the insult all the more caustic.

"I believe in individual examples," Morlac replied, but without conviction.

His cheeks were red, with shame, with fury, there was no telling. The major left a long pause. A horse's footfalls could be heard on the cobblestones of the square, then everything fell silent.

"Let's have a serious talk, shall we? Now, let me tell you why you committed this act and why you want to disappear."

"I'm listening."

"After your convalescence you were evacuated to Paris. You lived there for a few months without working. Your pension was enough. Throughout this period there were many occasions when you could have established contact with activists. But you didn't. If you were so preoccupied with a revolution, it would be fair to assume you would have grasped the opportunity of being in the capital to sign yourself up."

"How do you know this?"

"It's simple. When I was appointed to investigate your case, headquarters sent me your file. Veterans from the Eastern Front are fairly closely monitored by the police. Your friendliness with Russian soldiers didn't go unnoticed, would you believe. On your return, the intelligence services made sure you didn't have any undesirable contacts."

Morlac shrugged his shoulders but made no contradiction.

"You arrived here on June 15. You took up residence with a widow who hires out rooms. You proved very discreet. You didn't even go to see your brother-in-law who's taken over your family farm."

"I don't like him and the feeling's mutual. He's lazy and a thief."

"I'm not passing judgment. Just stating a fact. On the other hand, you frequently went to see your son."

This came as a bolt out of the blue and Morlac couldn't disguise his surprise.

"You hid so that you could watch him. One day you tried to talk to him and you frightened him. You still came back, though, but now you were even more cautious."

"So what? That's not a crime."

"Who said anything about a crime? Once again, I'm not passing judgment. I'm trying to understand."

"What is there to understand? He's my son, I want to see him, that's all there is to it."

"Of course. But why not see his mother?"

"We had a . . . misunderstanding."

"Oh, well said! Now, you see, Morlac, you're an intelligent man but I'm afraid that here, as with many other things, you're lying to yourself."

Lantier stood up and opened the window wide. There were no bars across it and, outside, Dujeux stepped forward to see what was going on. The major waved him away and leaned against the windowsill, looking out over the square. The dog, still in the same place, had sat up on his haunches.

"You're very unfair to that poor animal," the major said thoughtfully. "You resent him for his faithfulness. You say it's a stupid, animal quality. But we all have it in us, starting with you."

He turned toward Morlac and added, "In fact, you value this quality so highly that you've never forgiven Valentine for lacking in it. You're the most faithful man I know. And the proof is that you haven't forsaken the love you feel for her. It was for her that you came back here, wasn't it?"

Morlac shrugged again. He was looking at his hands.

"I think the real difference between us and animals," the major went on, "isn't faithfulness. The more strictly human characteristic that they completely lack is a different emotion, and one that you have as it happens."

"What's that?"

"Pride."

Lantier had hit the mark and Morlac might well have been a veteran who'd faced many ordeals, but his self-assurance was crumbling.

"You opted instead to punish her and punish yourself

by staging this simulated rebellion under her nose, rather than talking to her and finding out the truth."

"It wasn't simulated."

"Either way, it was tailor-made for her. It was her you were doing it for."

Morlac attempted one last objection but Lantier had cut off his access to pride because of what he'd said, so the prisoner's words were pronounced without the tone of voice that would have given them any menace.

"Good for her if she got the message."

"Unfortunately, you didn't hear her reply."

The sound of children playing reached them, coming from a neighboring yard. The hot, still air seemed to carry only high sounds, like the chapel bell which rang every quarter of an hour.

"In any event," Lantier concluded firmly, "I won't be an accomplice to your provocation. As I am expected to punish you, I know what punishment I shall inflict upon you. And it is one which will most hurt your pride. You're going to go and see her, and listen to her. Listen right to the end, and gauge how wrong you were. That will be your condemnation. But beware! I won't accept any prevarication."

"Do I have the option to refuse?"

"No."

One by one Lantier did up the buttons on his vest that he'd left open during the interview. He picked up his jacket, which he'd draped over the back of the chair behind the desk, and put it on. He ran his hand through his hair to tidy it, and smoothed his narrow moustache. He stood up tall, resuming the bearing typical of an officer.

"This case is closed. I won't hear any of your objections."

But this assertiveness masked a coyness, a shyness connected to what he had decided to say before he left. He was no longer a military investigating officer but just another ordinary man when he added:

"And now, actually, well . . . I have a favor to ask you."

CHAPTER X

The military investigating officer had gone straight back to his hotel because he knew Valentine was waiting for him there.

She was in the large lounge, sitting self-consciously under a vast painting depicting a stagecoach. She'd positioned herself near the right-hand corner, where the artist had put a country inn, as if she found the company of farmers' wives on their doorsteps less intimidating than the fine women peering out of the coach. She jumped to her feet when she saw the officer.

"Well?" she asked, taking his hands.

"Go and see him straightaway. He's expecting you."

And, as he climbed the stairs without looking back so as not to witness the young woman's emotion and perhaps also to hide his own, he added:

"He's a free man."

CHAPTER XI

The car threaded its way across the countryside. It was a military sedan with big chrome headlights and glossy black mudguards. The sun was warming the hood and Lantier had lowered the windscreen to get some air.

He drove through villages to the cries of children, and raised his hat to greet men working in the fields. Storms had raged the previous day and they had to be quick to harvest the last parcels of wheat. The smell of autumn was already in the air, and in places the woods were adopting their first hints of brown.

He'd wanted to travel in civilian clothes, to start getting used to this new life that was beginning. After Orléans he was impatient to reach Paris, and be reunited with his wife and children. How would they take the present he had for them? It was easier convincing himself they'd be happy just seeing him happy. Because, truth be told, it wasn't a very handsome present. And Morlac hadn't made any fuss about handing it over to him . . .

Every now and then Lantier turned toward the rear seat and glanced over to check: No, it really wasn't a very handsome present. Or rather it was to himself that he was offering it.

He reached out his arm and felt the old jowls with his hand.

"Isn't that right, Wilhelm?" he whooped.

And the dog seemed to be smiling, too.

A Tribute

It was in 2011. A French weekly had sent me to Jordan to cover the Arab Spring. Unfortunately for me, this was the only country where absolutely nothing was happening. I had the photographer Benoît Gysembergh with me, and we spent our time sipping beers and telling each other stories.

Benoît was a very talented man with a lot of imagination. His life had allowed him to witness much of the century and to watch at close quarters many eminently book-worthy events.

And yet of all the adventures he described to me during those leisurely days, I've remembered only one. It was a very short, simple anecdote, but I immediately sensed that it constituted one of those rare tiny crystals of life from which the edifice of a whole book can be built.

This story was about his grandfather. He returned a hero from the Great War and was decorated with the Légion d'honneur, but after having a few drinks one day he committed what was at the time an unprecedented act, a transgression which led to his an arrest and a trial. It is this episode that is recreated at the end of this book.

I never stopped thinking about Benoît as I wrote this book. His illness was diagnosed while I was writing. Sadly, he never read the book because sickness claimed him just as I was finishing it.

I only had time to tell him I would dedicate it to him.

These pages are for him, for his memory.
He was a dear friend and a great photographer.

ABOUT THE AUTHOR

Jean-Christophe Rufin is one of the founders of Doctors Without Borders and a former Ambassador of France in Senegal. He has written numerous best-sellers, including *The Abyssinian*, for which he won the Goncourt Prize for a debut novel in 1997. He also won the Goncourt Prize in 2001 for *Brazil Red*. He is the author of *The Dream Maker* (Europa Editions, 2013).